Sherlock Holmes and The Murder at The Savoy

and Other Stories

By

Mike Hogan

Published in the UK by MX Publishing
335 Princess Park Manor, Royal Drive,
London, N11 3GX
www.mxpublishing.co.uk

Cover images by Richard C Plaza
Cover design by www.staunch.com

Contents

One little Maid from School   1
Murder at the Savoy   42
A Scandal in Tite Street   92
Trial by Jury   134
The Moving Finger Writes   177

Forward

What cultural icons personify the Victorian era better than Sherlock Holmes and Doctor Watson and Gilbert and Sullivan? That they would have known each other is highly probable. Holmes was a music lover of course, and Gilbert was quarrelsome and litigious enough to need investigative help. Directly and indirectly through the music of the operettas, the worlds of Gilbert and Sullivan and Holmes and Watson meet in these stories.

One Little Maid from School

"Watson, wake up. We are there."

I blinked awake as the train screeched across a set of points, slowed as it entered Guildford station and stopped in a cloud of steam and smoke.

"At last a proper case, with no nonsense of ghouls or mummies about it," said Holmes, smiling and rubbing his hands together as he stepped onto the platform in his brown tweed suit and deerstalker hat. "A straightforward missing person's case with not a poltergeist in sight."

I climbed out of the carriage behind Holmes, leaving a pile of crumpled newspapers on the floor as the usual debris of rail travel à la Sherlock Holmes. "I say my dear fellow, must you wear that ridiculous deerstalker hat? We are not in the Highlands; we are less than thirty miles from Charing Cross."

Holmes laughed. "No spectres, mummies, sprites or — good Lord."

"Have you seen a sprite, Holmes?" I gathered our bags, batted away a small boy selling religious tracts and looked up. Holmes was staring along the platform with a half-smile on his face. I followed his gaze and saw a young man in a smart grey suit and blue homburg walking towards us with a purposeful air. He stopped before Holmes and held out his hand.

"Mr Holmes, good to see you again."

"Mr Barker. What are you doing here?"

"Same as you, sir. The Aylescombe Grange business. I understand that you act for Mr Percival Lavery, the stepfather. I was called in by his brother Mr August Lavery, the girl's step-uncle, as it were. "

"How did you —" Holmes checked himself.

Mr Barker smiled. "It's our business to know, sir."

"Let me introduce my friend, Doctor John Watson," said Holmes. "Watson, this is Archibald Barker, my rival on the Surrey side of the River."

"Hardly a rival, Mr Holmes," said Mr Barker as he shook my hand. "I am rarely called in on cases concerning the Quality. But you must admit that you are on my territory now, sir, for we are indeed in Surrey."

"Among the Quality, however," Holmes answered with a tight smile. "Aylescombe Grange School is reputedly very exclusive."

"The school will accept only the most eligible young ladies, sir, aged between sixteen and twenty-one; the curriculum focusses on subjects that will prepare them for married life: deportment, fashion, elegant chit-chat at table and so on."

Mr Barker smiled an engaging smile. "Have you booked a hotel, gentlemen? If not, I can recommend the Angel Hotel on the Portsmouth Road where I am put up. I took the liberty of reserving you a room as the town is packed for market day and lodgings are main hard to come by. We can't have Mr Sherlock Holmes mouldering in a stable, can we now? I have a carriage in the station forecourt if I may offer a lift."

"That's kind of you, Mr Barker," said Holmes with a nod to me. "That would suit us very well."

We followed Mr Barker out of the station to where he had parked his dogcart under the supervision of a common loafer. We clambered aboard, Mr Barker took the reins and we set off at a walk.

"What a beautiful spring day, Holmes," I exclaimed as we passed banks of daffodils on either side of the station approach road. "Isn't it fine to be out of the smoke and bustle of the city and in one of our fine old country towns? A poster at the station showed a Norman castle that I shall take the opportunity of visiting. And the market is one of the oldest chartered in England."

"You say the uncle of the missing girl has commissioned you to find her?" Holmes asked.

"Step-uncle, if I may use the term," Mr Barker replied. "He is no direct relation. Your client, Mr Percival Lavery, married the girl's widowed mother, so he is no blood relation neither. Percival and his brother August are on bad terms; they do not speak."

"Eleanor is just twenty, as I understand it."

"That is correct, sir. She disappeared on the night of her twentieth birthday-eve, on Thursday, the day before yesterday. My client, her Uncle August, had visited the Grange earlier that day and he spoke with Eleanor. He returned the following morning, but the girl was not to be found. Uncle August telegraphed me, and I was on the case by lunchtime."

"You have acted for the uncle on previous occasions?" Holmes asked in a tentative tone.

"I have, sir. Mr Lavery owns a cab company in the Old Kent Road and he has an interest in several omnibus lines. I have appeared as his agent in one or two little matters. I break no confidence — it is generally known — when I say that my client is a strong-willed man, that he will brook no gain-say and that he is dangerous when crossed. It takes a firm hand to run a cab business."

Holmes nodded. "Was Uncle August a frequent visitor to the Grange, I wonder?"

"Monthly at the very least; he is a doting step-uncle," Mr Barker answered with a lewd wink. "There is a photograph of Eleanor in that bag at Doctor Watson's feet."

I leant down, opened the bag and took out a court-sized portrait of a startlingly beautiful young girl in a kimono with her hair made up in the Japanese style. I handed it to Holmes.

3

"She is one of the 'Three Little Maids', gentlemen," said Mr Barker. "She plays Pitti-Sing in the school production of *The Mikado* at the end of term." He chuckled. "If we find her, that is."

Holmes handed me back the photograph. "What of the father, my client?"

"I rather left him to you, sir."

"He has a racing stable near Newmarket," said Holmes. "He was under investigation in the Derby fixing affair of last year, but nothing came of it. The telegram requesting that I act for Mr Lavery came from Paris."

I sniffed. "Paris? The girl's relations are of a somewhat louche character, Holmes."

"And young Eleanor's money?" Holmes asked. "I presume the step-uncle's solicitude and the step-father's concern do not derive wholly from familial motives."

"She is a twenty-thousand pounder, at the least, Mr Holmes," said Mr Barker. "All in copper-bottomed stock and tightly entailed by her father's will, despite Mr Percival's attempts to break it. That's according to Mr August. He claims that Percival would marry the girl himself if the law did not forbid it. He further claims that Percival intends that she shall never marry; not in his lifetime while he controls the interest on her capital."

"Monstrous," I exclaimed.

Holmes pursed his lips. "A man may marry his step-niece. Uncle August has a clear field, once she is of age."

"So I am given to understand," Mr Barker said. "I believe he is already staking his claim, and aiming to bind the girl to his will."

"A frightful business, Holmes," I said. "The man should be horse whipped."

The dog cart halted in a leafy lane at the top of a hill. "Here is your castle, Doctor," Mr Barker said, pointing to a tall ruined building in a landscaped garden. "I took a roundabout route to give you a view. The local authorities are turning the grounds into a park."

"I say, Holmes, have we time to —"

Holmes regarded the ruins with blank indifference, and we drove on.

The Angel Hotel was a fine Elizabethan-looking coaching inn with white walls inset with thick brown beams. We clattered through an arch and stopped in a large cobbled yard. A stable boy led the horse and carriage away. Servants took our luggage and showed us into the lobby, a large room panelled in dark wood with a gallery and upper floors reached by an elegant staircase. Brass urns containing ferns and rubber plants stood on tables along the walls, and antlers and other hunting paraphernalia hung from the gallery.

"May I cordially invite you and Doctor Watson to luncheon?" Mr Barker asked. "You are on my ground, gentlemen, so I will accept no refusal. I have ordered a noble turbot fresh by railway from the South Coast."

Holmes bowed assent for both of us and we said our adieus.

After the usual formalities, Holmes and I were shown upstairs by a page. Our room was a pleasant, if cramped, chamber, with just enough space for a pair of four-poster beds jammed against each other below a small window. Two upright chairs, a marble-topped washstand and a tall wardrobe completed the furnishings. A single bright note among the sober browns was a bowl of fresh-cut daffodils and primroses that stood on the washstand.

I picked a primrose as a buttonhole.

"You will be taken for a Little Disraeliite, Watson. We may be stoned in the streets."

"There is no such organisation, Holmes; you are thinking of the Primrose League. And Guildford is staunchly conservative. I will be feted by an admiring populace."

I unpacked the few necessities that I had brought with me. I prided myself, as an old campaigner, on travelling light. "Mr Barker seems an affable sort, if perhaps a little forward. I have heard you mention his name a number of times, usually in a pejorative context."

"Nonsense," said Holmes as he delved in his bag.

"You call him your arch-rival on the Surrey side."

"A whimsical reference. He poses no threat to my practice. He finds his clientele among the costermongers, railway workers and low garment traders of the Borough and Camberwell. His office is in the basement of a house in St George's Road in Lambeth where he lives with his mother. She takes in lodgers. The house is just by the Bedlam lunatic asylum and the Catholic cathedral, convenient for visitors to either or both establishments."

I laid my nightclothes on the end of the bed. "Mr Barker is a consulting detective?"

Holmes chuckled. "Hardly, he is little more than a private enquiry agent. His last case exposed an errant husband who dallied with a shop girl at an oil merchant's on the Brixton Road."

I frowned. "Did not your last case involve a one-legged publican who —"

"I number many of the crowned heads of Europe among my clients, my dear fellow," Holmes replied in a stiff tone. "There is no comparison."

I counted on my fingers. "And a railway porter, a footman, a distressed clergyman, a lady assistant at a bar on the Underground Railway —"

6

"My clients form an eclectic, but select group. The bathroom is at the end of the corridor, I expect." Holmes tossed a coin.

"Heads," I called.

He pocketed the coin and picked up his sponge bag. "I take first dibs. I shall not be long; I bathed very thoroughly but the day before yesterday."

We joined Mr Barker downstairs at a small table in a window alcove, ordered whiskies with soda and chatted amiably. He then led us in to luncheon and we shared a fine turbot accompanied with a dry white wine. After cherry trifle for pudding, we ordered coffee and I offered Holmes and Mr Barker cigars from my case.

"The school?" Holmes asked as he lit his cigar.

"Aylescombe Grange is a couple of miles from here," Mr Barker answered. "It is a rambling old house with extensive gardens and playing fields. I took the liberty of noting the details of the staff for you Mr Holmes — saves you some time."

He passed Holmes a note.

"You are too kind, Mr Barker," Holmes said in a tight tone.

"Call it a professional courtesy, sir. And perhaps a slight expression of my admiration of your deductive skills. The Maupertuis case, sir, and the matter of the devil Ricoletti! What can I say, other than I model my methods on yours in every particular? I thought, despite our antipathetic clients, that we might work together in the matter; we might cooperate, as they say."

"Do they?" Holmes answered coldly.

"You have been active in your short time in Guildford, Mr Barker," I said, to break the long silence that followed.

"I try to make up for my lack of detective skills by the practice of indefatigability, Doctor — sweat and hard labour.

Ah, here is Sergeant Callan. He said that he might be able to join us for coffee if the trains from London connected well."

Sergeant Callan of Scotland Yard, an elderly man in a rumpled black suit and bowler, and, according to Holmes, something of a plodder, spotted us and joined us at our table. "Mr Holmes, Doctor. Good to see you again. And you too, Archie, I got your wire and I have your item out in the stables. Inspector Lestrade send regrets and best wishes, as he is still busy with the clerical impersonation and fraud case in Frinton."

"Can I tempt you to take something from the menu, Sergeant?" said Mr Barker.

"No, thanks, I had my dinner at the station in London. I have something for you too, Mr Holmes, from Inspector Dubugue, of the Sûreté in Paris." Callan passed Holmes a cablegram.

Holmes waved the form to me. "Dubugue says that Mr Percival Lavery arrived at Calais on Thursday evening," I said. "He stays at the Hôtel d'Alsace with a young lady that he characterises as his niece. I say, Holmes, Miss Eleanor disappeared the previous night. She must therefore be in Paris, with her step-father."

"I'll tell you what, Archie, those meringues look tasty," said Callan. "I might try one."

I frowned. "But why take her away in such a dramatic fashion, when he could have arranged the matter very simply with the school principal?"

Holmes smiled and raised an eyebrow at Barker.

"I have obtained an audience with Madame Tench, the principal of the school for four o'clock this afternoon," Mr Barker said with a smile. "Perhaps you would like to join me, gentlemen; the lady is difficult to get to see."

8

Holmes and I retired to the Smoking Room after lunch and caught up with the news in the London papers. There was nothing yet of the Aylescombe Grange affair.

"We might go for a short walk," said Holmes. "You are out of tobacco."

I heard a tremendous rumble and clatter of hooves and looked up as a mail coach thundered through the arch and into the inn yard. "I say, Holmes, isn't she a beauty? How nostalgic; it's like being in a Dickens novel. Shall we have a look?"

Holmes followed me out into the yard. The coach, a splendid four-horse yellow and black affair with high springs, was heavily loaded with a dozen or so passengers. We watched as they climbed out or clambered down from the box, tired and cramped, but well-pleased with their adventure.

"From London?" I asked a bewhiskered clerical gentleman as he consulted his watch.

"Indeed, sir. We left the White Horse Cellars in Piccadilly at eleven and three minutes, and I set my foot in the stable yard of the Angel, Guildford at two fifty-six in the afternoon. We would have done better had it not been for a wilful dray at Ripley that cost us fourteen minutes and eleven seconds. Better than seven miles in an hour, sir, with no fuss of crowded stations and ticket queues; no sooty smuts and grubby carriages; no charging across the countryside at a frantic pace peering out of grimy windows at sights that flash by faster than the human eye can comprehend. No, sir: I travel as our forefathers did; it's the mail coach for me, and a glorious spring day to boot."

"I envy you."

He smiled. "You need not do so, sir. For ten shillings inside, or twelve and six on the box, you may emulate us. Think of it, my dear sir: the open road. Apply to the gentleman in the high hat; he is Mr Thorogood, our driver. And now, if I may, I shall wish you a very good day and repair inside for a glass of the local brew and something to refresh the inner man."

The gentleman tipped his hat to me and I to him.

I watched as the spent team were replaced with fine, fresh horses. A boy handed me a pamphlet that gave the *New Times* mail coach schedule, and confirmed the reverend gentleman's prices.

Holmes joined me. "I say, my dear fellow," I said, "the mail coach driver, Mr Thorogood engages to leave *The Angel* in the afternoon and to reach Piccadilly by seven in the evening. It is a regular daily service. Might we tentatively book two outsides for the day after tomorrow? Twenty-four hours should see an end to the case, wouldn't you agree? The girl has been spirited away to Paris by her step-father. Think of it, Holmes, the open road! What do you say? What's the matter, my dear friend? Why so gloomy?"

"Barker has got Toby, the hound."

"Who is Toby?"

"I told you, Watson; do keep up."

I looked at Holmes in bewilderment. "What has Mr Barker done that you abuse him so?"

"Toby is the hound, not Barker; although I have cause to — never mind. Toby is the dog I use from time to time to follow a trail. Callan brought him down from London for Barker."

I pursed my lips. "You should be grateful, Holmes. You have been saved the dog rental. As you are working together, cooperating, as Mr Barker put it, it's of no consequence which of you finds the missing girl." Holmes growled an unintelligible reply, and I hid my mischievous grin behind my pamphlet.

Mr Barker joined us in the yard. "High words are coming from the Smoking Room, gentlemen. Mr Percival Lavery is back from Paris with his niece, and he and Mr August Lavery have broken their bond of silence. They are making up for lost years of silent reproach by yelling at the top of their voices. From what I can gather, each brother accuses the other of absconding with the girl."

I frowned. "I do not understand. Mr Percival Lavery has brought his niece back to Guildford from France. How then could the brother August have absconded with her?"

Mr Barker smiled and led Holmes and I under the arch, out into the Portsmouth Road, and back into the Angel by the main door. The sound of loud contention came from the Smoking Room to our right. We could see through the open doorway that two gentlemen were having a blazing row. "Mutton-chop whiskers is my man," said Mr Barker. "Balding with walrus moustache is yours. And the lady in the hat in the lobby purports to be Mr Percival's niece."

I looked across the lobby and saw a woman seated on a sofa reading a magazine. She wore a pale-yellow ensemble, with a black feather boa around her neck. On her head was a gigantic yellow hat heaped with primroses, stuffed canaries and bright feathers. She seemed impervious to the clamour coming from the Smoking Room. She turned a page, looked up and saw Holmes, Barker and myself in the doorway. She fluttered her eyelashes, smiled and turned back to her magazine.

Holmes sniffed. "*Eau de Cologne Impériale* by Guerlain of Paris. The lady is particular, but she is not Eleanor Lavery."

We climbed aboard Mr Barker's dogcart once again and set off through the town and into pleasant country. Sergeant Callan sat next to me, and the dog, Toby, sat between Mr Barker and Holmes looking bright-eyed and cheerful.

"Should we not have made our number with our client before we left, Holmes?" I asked.

"He was otherwise engaged."

We arrived at the imposing gates of Aylescombe Grange just before four. A gatekeeper let us through, and we followed a winding gravel driveway past woodland on our left and open grassland and a large lake on our right. The house came into sight. It was a long, dark, ivy-covered neo-Gothic building, with a tall central clock tower and a wing on the right in a red-brick Georgian style that was clearly a recent addition.

"The previous owner, the Principal's uncle, was a geologist," said Mr Barker following my gaze and playing Holmes' mind-reading trick. "He built the new wing to house his fossil collection and promptly died, leaving the Grange to his sister, Madame Tench. The rocks are in a pile by the stables."

As we neared the Grange, we passed a field in which a group of young ladies in white smocks practised physical jerks. A tall, thin lady in tweeds led the formation. She blew her whistle repeatedly to regain the attention of the girls as they turned and followed the progress of our carriage up the drive. Some girls had the impertinence to wave, and Barker gave evidence of a lack of gentlemanly decorum by waving back.

We stopped under a stone portico, and an elderly butler, who introduced himself as Rutledge, led us through a huge hall hung with more armour and ancient weaponry than I would have thought appropriate for a select girls' school. The wood panelling, weapons and stuffed stags' heads on the walls gave the room a gloomy atmosphere. We followed Rutledge up a long, curving staircase and along a forbiddingly dark corridor hung with sombre portraits to a small reception room furnished with bright sofas and occasional tables. Two young girls in their late-teens wearing blue and white uniforms sat huddled together on a sofa. One was a graceful and pretty auburn-haired girl, and the other was a plump blonde young lady who wore glasses. They regarded us with unrestrained interest. The auburn-haired girl asked politely whether Toby might be petted. Mr Barker smiled an impertinent smile and let the dog off his leash. The girls instantly smothered him with pats, hugs and even kisses. I looked away in embarrassment just as a door opened in the panelled walls and a short, grey-haired lady in brown tweeds appeared in the doorway.

"Estelle and Margaret, release that dog instantly and report to sister for a thorough wash. Return here when you are clean and ladylike again."

The girls slipped out, and Callan grabbed Toby and clipped on his lead.

"I am Madame Tench, the school principal," the lady said. "Kindly tie up that dog and follow me into my office."

We sat in a row before the Principal's desk. Despite the lady's gender, I was irresistibly reminded of my own schooldays. Madame Tench's office, with its dark panelling, busts of famous people and rows of leather-bound books on tall shelves, was a copy of the headmaster's office at my school. Even the dry, leathery smell was the same. Holmes smiled at me and nodded; he was of the same mind.

Callan made the introductions and explained that he was acting in his official capacity on a complaint of kidnapping laid by Mr Percival Lavery against his brother, Mr August Lavery.

"Aylescombe Grange is a school for young ladies from the very best families in the land," Madame Tench replied. "The Earl of Heathermere and Sir Septimus Froud have confided their daughters into my care. I can assure you, sirs, that no incident of the criminal type that you describe could occur at the Grange. You suggest that Eleanor has been kidnapped. I say poppycock."

"Eleanor Lavery is missing, Madame. If not kidnapped, then what?" Callan asked in a tight tone.

Madame Tench sniffed. "She has run away. We provide guidance to young ladies from sixteen to twenty-two. That is a volatile age, and the girls get all sorts of nonsense into their heads — well, some girls. I may say without fear of contradiction that Eleanor is a frothy, flighty girl with little bottom; I mean that in its sense of foundation or solidity, of course."

She pursed her lips. "I admit that her circumstances are pitiable. She lost her father to disease in India when she was a baby, and then her mother three years ago in a carriage accident; that was just a year after her mother's marriage to Mr Percival Lavery. In the circumstances, Mr Lavery thought it wise to enrol her at Aylescombe Grange."

Callan consulted his notes. "Eleanor was not in her bed on Thursday morning when the girls were roused to attend assembly and Divine Service. Her bed had not been slept in."

"That is so."

"Are the ladies not checked during the night?"

"Madame Frazelle was Duty Mistress that night. She had imbibed rather too much cherry brandy after dinner, and she fell asleep. She is from Jersey, in the Channel Islands, you understand." Madame Tench raised her eyebrows. "Her father is one of our school governors."

I frowned at a large wooden cabinet with polished brass fittings that stood next to Madame Tench's desk, and in front of my chair. It had several rows of small circular windows, with small holes under each one. The names of rooms in the building, such as Library and Kitchen were written on labels pasted above the windows.

Madame Tench followed my gaze and smiled. "It is a telephonic apparatus of the latest design, Doctor. I had it installed some six months ago when I learned that the German Emperor, on a visit to Buckingham Palace, used a similar apparatus to contact the Palace Mews and inquire daily on the health of his charger. The horse was evidently a sensitive beast, and unused to travel outside the boundaries of the German Empire. The Channel crossing had distressed it. What a fine fellow the Kaiser must be to show such delicate feeling for his horse. His bust is on that bookshelf behind you, next to that of Nelson.

"I use the telephonic equipment to effect instant communication with the various departments of the school," she continued in a business-like tone. "We had voice pipes at one time, but they were used by mice as runs and nesting places. We are plagued by the beasts, although we have a veritable nuisance of cats."

She picked up a plug with a short wire attached. "If I wish to communicate with, for example, the kitchens I simply push this plug into the hole below the window so labelled, pick up the earpiece and turn this small handle, thus. A bell rings in the kitchen. Cook picks up the earpiece of her apparatus and speaks into a horn — oh, hello Mrs Bellamy, no I am demonstrating the telephonic apparatus. What? The ham again? Come and see me at five o'clock." Madame Tench replaced her earpiece, pulled out the kitchen plug and tut-tutted. "The tricks these girls get up to."

She regained her composure and continued. "A young lady must be *au fait* with the latest developments, not only in art and music, but also with modern invention; we live in an innovative age, gentlemen." She shook her head. "Where, I ask you, would we be without Mr Hiram Maxim's hair tongs? At Aylescombe we pride ourselves on keeping up-to-date in such matters; it is one of the points that I emphasise with prospective clients."

Sergeant Callan leaned forward impatiently. "I understand that Mr August Lavery, Eleanor's step-uncle, spoke to his step-niece on the day before she went missing, Madame. Do you know the tenor of that conversation?"

Madame Tench pursed her lips. "I do not. Mr August Lavery has always been most attentive to his step-niece; he writes to me regularly regarding the girl's health and scholastic progress."

She smiled. "He has made a considerable contribution to the expenses of our little drama this term. We are putting on *The Mikado*, with full permissions from Mr D'Oyly Carte, of course, as a change from Shakespeare. Mr Lavery paid for the sets and certain foundation garments necessitated by the Japanese costumes. Uncle August requires that Eleanor wear only white when he comes to visit; such a pretty notion."

"And the step-father, Mr Percival Lavery?" asked Holmes.

Madame Tench frowned. "He came to the Grange only once, to make the necessary arrangements for the young lady to join us. However, the fee cheques arrive regularly; he banks with Coutts, a solid firm."

"Might we view the young lady's bedroom, Madame?" Callan asked.

Madame Tench bridled. "Is that necessary? Men are not admitted to the dormitories under any circumstances whatsoever."

"I am afraid I must insist," said Callan, standing up and wincing from a spasm of back pain. "This is a police matter."

Madame Tench led Holmes, Barker, Callan and I out of her office and up the central staircase of the building. As we climbed the stairs, a line of young ladies in diaphanous Grecian costumes passed us going down. Each had a small pile of books balanced on her head. I smoothed my moustache and was put entirely out of countenance when one of the young ladies winked at me. Or perhaps at Holmes, or more likely at me. No, definitely at me.

"Good posture," I said to Holmes, "is an important aspiration for a young person."

"Quite right, Doctor," said Madame Tench firmly.

We followed her along a corridor and into a large, bright room lined with beds and lockers. "This is Gordon House; Wellington is on the next floor, and Clive and Cromwell are in the New Wing."

Holmes prowled along a line of beds and stopped at one on the right. "Here is the young lady's bed, and that is her locker."

Madame Tench frowned. "How did you know?"

Holmes raised an eyebrow at Barker.

"All the other lockers have dolls or stuffed toys on top," Barker said. "Only that locker is clear."

"Ah," said Madame Tench, "I thought Mr Holmes had done something clever. Eleanor took her stuffed rabbit with her. What kind of abduction is that, Sergeant? What abductee would be allowed to take along her toys?"

Callan breathed deeply as he recovered his breath from the stair climb. "Would you mind opening the locker, Madame?"

"It is not locked."

Holmes and Barker knelt and laid the contents of the locker on the bed: a hockey stick, a pile of clothes, a Bible, a science textbook, a life of General Gordon and a Bradshaw. Holmes pounced on the Bradshaw before Barker could grab it.

"What would a young lady need with a railway timetable?" Holmes asked.

"I have no idea how she came by it," exclaimed Madame Tench with a frown. "I keep Bradshaw in my office, naturally, but not in the girls' library. They have no need of railway timetables. And all private book purchases must be approved by me. I have no idea how Eleanor may have come by the book."

"Here is also an odd book for a young girl to have in her possession," I said, holding up the textbook. It is 'A Guide to Telephonic Communication'."

I passed it to Holmes, and he flipped through it. "Wires and mouthpieces, no spirits or astral planes. Did the girl have a scientific bent, I wonder? Aha!"

Holmes held up an unopened letter. "This was used as a bookmark, or perhaps hidden in the book." He turned to Madame Tench. "Do you read letters that come for the girls in your charge?"

She drew herself up to her full, if diminutive height. "I do not. I am constrained by the law. Stamped letters are the property of the Crown until delivered to their recipient; they must not be tampered with."

I nodded. "Quite right, Madam."

"Outgoing correspondence is another matter; I read the girls' letters to ensure that the grammar and vocabulary they employ are a credit to the School, and that the sentiments expressed are suitable for young ladies of good family."

"This envelope is addressed to Miss E Lavery," said Holmes. "To be called for at the local post office. Printed on the back is the address of Liberty's Emporium of decorative items and Japanese apparel in London. The envelope is glued not wafer- or wax-sealed. Eleanor knew what the contents were, and did not bother to open it. It is very probably, judging from the flimsiness of the paper inside, as felt through the envelope, a receipt or a bill; perhaps a receipt for something chosen by her, but paid for by another, or a bill that the young lady wished away."

"Perhaps it came after her disappearance, Holmes," I suggested.

"A foul calumny on the English postal service, Watson! It was posted on Monday. It arrived on Tuesday, or Wednesday at the latest."

Callan stood to attention. "I will take it upon myself, as the only official of the Crown present, to open the letter and view the contents. I will require your signatures, Madame and gentlemen, as witnesses to my action."

"Good man, Sergeant," said Holmes.

"Stout fellow," I exclaimed.

He opened the letter and read the enclosure. "The cover note is from Liberty's in Regent Street, London. Attached is a receipt for five guineas for a pair of *basques* of Japanese silk."

I looked from Holmes to Callan and received blank looks.

"It is an article of dress," said Madame Tench stiffly. "Of ladies' dress; an undergarment of an intimate character, completely unsuitable for the young ladies in this establishment."

I reddened and looked at my toes.

"How did she pay for it?" she asked. "Not in cash. I control the young ladies' accounts, and I can assure you, gentleman, that no girl in this establishment has access to such a large amount. It would be too great a temptation to sin."

There was a knock at the door and a pale-faced police constable entered. He handed Callan a note.

Callan stood. "Madame, gentlemen, if you will excuse me?" He hurried out, followed by the policeman.

"You expressed the view that Eleanor might have run away, Madame Tench," Holmes asked. "Was she upset about anything recently?"

"No, not that I had heard. She is a flighty girl, but not prone to moping."

"And where do you think she might have run to? Her step-father's home perhaps?"

"Possibly. There is a cousin in Cornwall. I telegraphed her this morning and I have not yet received a reply."

Barker slipped across to a window; he nodded to me and I joined him. We looked down to the front lawn and the lake beyond. A group of uniformed police were gathered at the lake. Callan was with them gesticulating.

"I'll get Toby," Barker said.

I turned to Holmes. "I say, something is up."

We reached the lakeshore as a party of police constables equipped with poles boarded a half-dozen punts.

"We are dragging the lake," said Callan as we came up.

"Why?" Holmes asked.

Callan ushered us to a spot on the lakeshore under the shade a huge weeping willow. A small pile of clothes lay at the water's edge.

"Identified as Miss Eleanor's, Mr Holmes. And including this." He held up a flimsy silk and lace confection with a bodice and flared waist.

"A *basque*, I make no doubt; from Liberty's."

"It bears their label, sir. It was identified as Eleanor's by that girl under the tree."

The shorter, chubby, blond girl from Madame Tench's waiting room stood under the willow, quietly weeping.

Callan shaded his eyes with his hand and surveyed the expanse of the lake. "We're going to need help."

I looked at the white clothes on the lakeshore, took off my primrose nosegay and threw it into the water. "What a horrible waste of a young life, Holmes. I should like to horsewhip Uncle August."

Holmes turned to me.

"Do not, as some ungracious pastors do,
Show me the steep and thorny way to heaven,
Whiles, like a puff' d and reckless libertine,
Himself the primrose path of dalliance treads."

"I say, Holmes. Show a little respect."

"Come, we must speak with Eleanor's friends," he answered.

Barker passed us with Toby on a leash as we hurried back to the Grange.

A hugely fat lady with a fierce expression and plump, folded arms stood with Madame Tench under the portico.

"No, Mrs Bellamy, we shall let the girls promenade as usual after their tea," said Madame Tench. "I want no changes from our usual routine. They will peer from the windows if we pen them inside. Let them chatter as usual; it will clear the air."

She turned to us. "Ah, gentlemen. I understand that several items of Eleanor's clothes have been found by the lake."

"That is so," I answered heavily.

She nodded. "Well, then. As I told Cook, we shall continue our usual routine, unless some development occurs. In dry weather, the girls are allowed an hour's promenade on the front lawn after tea so that they may engage in light conversation. Let us move them to the back lawn for today, but allow the Promenade to go ahead. It will tire them. We may also allow the girls an extra cup of cocoa with their supper; it is an excellent soporific."

She bowed and retreated inside.

"Are you the Scotland Yard detectives, then?" the cook asked with an offensive leer.

"No, we are —" I began.

"Yes," said Holmes. "We are detectives."

"Then tell me this, if you can. Who is stealing my sausages?"

We followed Mrs Bellamy along back corridors and down several flights of stairs to the kitchen, a large basement room with the ovens, ranges, shelves of pots and pans, and long tables that one would expect in a boarding school kitchen.

She led us into a pantry and pointed to a glass-fronted cabinet.

"Right there they were, clear as daylight, when I cleaned up last night. When I came down to my kitchen after tea, I was missing a dozen cooked sausages and the butt end of a nice piece of ham that I was to slice paper thin for Madame Tench's sandwiches for late supper."

"Perhaps Miss Eleanor did not run away," I said. "Could she be hiding somewhere in the building?"

"Miss Eleanor?" the cook cried. "She eats like a sparrow, does Miss Eleanor. No, no, I'd not expect her to eat two pound of cooked sausages ready for a toad-in-the-hole the next morning and a fine butt end of ham. No, no, she pecked at her food, did Miss Eleanor, like a sparrow, really, or a jay."

"When were these cabinets last cleaned?'

The cook folded her arms and glared at Holmes. "What are you implying, you impertinent wretch?"

Holmes sighed and pointed to the finger prints on the glass of the top cabinet.

"Note well, Watson. The pudgy prints are a vital clue."

A high-pitched screech rent the air and Holmes nodded to me. "From the back of the house. Come!"

Another long scream was followed by a barrage of shrieks and squeals.

I followed Holmes at the run, up a set of stairs and along dingy corridors and out an open back door. A group of girls in school uniform wearing extravagant hats and holding frilly parasols were clustered together in a panic on the lawn. Several spotted Holmes and I and pointed up to the clock tower with their parasols.

I stopped and looked up. A small window at the very top of the tower was open, and I thought I saw a pale face, and then a hand.

A small shower of flowers fell over us. The girls screeched and clutched each other.

"Nobody is allowed in the Tower," said a sultry voice. "It's out-of-bounds."

I turned and saw that the voice belonged to the pretty, auburn-haired girl that had been in Madame Tench's office earlier.

"It must be Eleanor," said another voice.

"It's a man," said a third voice. "How could the ghost not be a man? It came into dorm once and asked me for a kiss."

"Mine asked me for the loan of thruppence," said a sad voice from back of the crowd.

"Then how could it be Eleanor?" another voice asked.

More flowers rained down. Toby bounded out of the back door and ran from group to group of girls sniffing their clothes as they squealed and screamed even louder.

"Great grief," said Holmes as Mr Barker appeared in the doorway. "No self-respecting ghost would subject itself to such a cacophony."

"I put him on the scent of her gym clothes," said Mr Barker.

"Let us to the Tower," Holmes said.

Mr Barker grabbed Toby, clipped on his lead and we followed Holmes back inside the Grange. The dog soon caught a strong scent, and we found a narrow staircase that looked promising. We pounded up the stairs into the Tower, past the clock mechanism, and up to a tiny square room at its apex. It was a wooden-floored pyramid lit by narrow windows in each wall.

Holmes and Mr Barker stood in the open doorway and each pulled out a magnifying glass. I took Toby's lead and watched as

23

they examined the room. I saw Mr Barker gingerly pick up a knife, and Holmes a stained scrap of lace.

"No apparitions," said Holmes after an intensive scrutiny of the room. "But we have a plethora of clues: bloodstains, several strands of black hair — Eleanor's colour of course — a broken chair, blood-stained lace and a bloody knife. It is very like the prop room of a third-rate repertory company doing a condensed version of *Hamlet*."

He bent and picked up some flowers from the floor. "Let me see: rosemary, pansies, fennel, columbines, rue, daisies, and violets, of course. Here, Watson, take another violet for your buttonhole.

> *"A violet in the youth of primy nature,*
> *Forward, not permanent- sweet, not lasting;*
> *The perfume and suppliance of a minute;*
> *No more."*

Holmes put a daisy in his own buttonhole and tossed one to Mr Barker. "Daisies are for deception; we are being played, gentlemen."

"Toby is still on a strong scent, sir," said Mr Barker.

Holmes nodded and Mr Barker let Toby drag him down the stairs. We followed at a more sedate pace.

"How did the apparition escape us, Holmes?" I asked. "We came up the only stairs."

Holmes tapped the wooden panelling of the stairwell. "I expect there are a dozen secret doors and staircases in this building. And the girls will have found them out. I know that we mere boys did at my school."

We reached the gloomy corridor at the bottom of the stairs. I turned to make a remark to Holmes, but he held up his hand.

"Come out."

A girl wearing school uniform with a huge, feathered hat set slantwise across her head and holding a frilly parasol emerged from the shadows. I recognised the auburn-haired girl from Madame Tench's office, and the back garden.

"Hello, Estelle," said Holmes.

The girl smiled and beckoned us to follow her along the corridor and out into a small courtyard lit by a single gas lamp high on the wall above. She set her hat at an even more seductive angle, leaned against the wall and twirled her parasol.

"I say, Holmes, is this quite proper?" I asked.

Estelle smiled. "May I have a cigarette?"

"You certainly may not," I exclaimed. Holmes clicked his fingers at me. I most reluctantly passed him my packet and he lit two cigarettes and handed one to Estelle in a gesture of dangerous intimacy.

"We walk on the lawn for an hour after tea during the Promenade," Estelle said in a sultry tone, taking a puff of the cigarette. "We are supposed to discuss appropriate topics — literature, fashion and the iniquity of servants. Of course we are all upset about Eleanor, and that is all we talk about." She sang softly.

> *"I mean to rule the earth,*
> *As he the sky--*
> *We really know our worth,*
> *The sun and I!*

Don't you love Yum-Yum? She is no blushing violet; she knows exactly what she wants and she means to have it."

Estelle leaned towards me and sniffed. "I like your primrose *boutonniere*, Doctor; it gives you a jaunty, devil-may-care look. But why have you not given it to a lucky girl? Eleanor was the prettiest, but you'd choose Maggie for money: she has a hundred thousand in Consols and her papa owns half Warwickshire. Do not doctors make heaps of money; I have heard that they do?"

"When did you notice that Eleanor was gone?" Holmes asked.

Estelle pouted, then smiled again. "Darling Eleanor? She'd gone when we woke up. Her bed was hardly slept in. Uncle Odious had pestered her with proposals the day before, and was to do so again on her birthday. I would have jumped straight into the lake at the prospect."

Holmes smiled. "You mean Uncle August."

"The fiend," I cried.

Estelle looked me up and down. "I see that you are not married, Doctor; you not wear a ring, and your socks are imperfect matches; both are black, but one is herringbone and the other plain. A good wife notices such things. I am of age in August, on the Glorious Twelfth.

From three little maids take one away.
Two little maids remain, and they
Won't have to wait very long, they say.
Three little maids from school."

She smiled a thin smile. "The hunt will then be on. A colonel of the guards, a friend of my father's, has offered his withered hand. He was wounded in the Mutiny. You have a military bearing, Doctor, but I expect that you are too young for the Mutiny."

I smoothed my moustache. "I was with the 66th at Maiwand."

She smiled. "Were you terribly brave? I am sure that you were. I noticed that you favour your leg. An honourable wound I make no doubt."

I bowed coldly.

Estelle sighed. "I should require my husband to be particularly brave; he should be in the forefront of any action. That is an absolute requirement, else how could one look the sergeants' wives in the face when one visits them to counsel economy and thrift in the ranks?"

She chuckled. "It is amusing really, don't you think, gentlemen? As the Colonel's lady, I will be obliged to give tips to the wives of the warrant officers on household management; yet my knowledge of life is confined to the correct wines to serve with pheasant, and how the napkins must be folded for a Royal Visit."

"Did Eleanor drown herself in the lake?" Holmes asked quietly.

Estelle blew a smoke ring across the courtyard. "It is possible. She was upset at not getting the plum part in *The Mikado*. Eleanor should have been Yum-Yum, mostly for the look of the thing, but also because she has a better voice than Maggie. Maggie's father is a benefactor to the School, of course; he paid for the new organ in the chapel."

She shrugged a most unladylike shrug. "*C'est la vie, n'est pas*? But Pitti-Sing performs the Raven Hair song, which is a fine one, and Eleanor had raven hair. Don't you remember the song, Doctor?"

She looked expectantly at me. I shook my head, and Estelle sang.

> *"Art and nature, thus allied,*
> *Go to make a pretty bride."*

"Ssshh!" I exclaimed.

She laughed. "What a prude your medical friend is, Mr Holmes. But you are a bohemian. Only a bohemian would venture into a girls' school in such a hat. It is an ear-flapped concoction of a peculiar sort that only the Antichrist might wear. We have a deep lake, sir, not just for errant virgins, but for errant hats."

"Holmes, the girl is in drink."

Estelle laughed. "Madame Frazelle's cherry brandy, Doctor. She has a large stock. I sang the Raven Hair song in front of the Prince of Wales when he visited my people at Dorford Castle, our country place. He was kind enough to give me a kiss on the cheek; his beard was deliciously ticklish."

"Holmes, I must protest —"

She turned to me and smiled. "You must understand that I am a New Woman, Doctor. The outmoded mores of Society do not apply to me. I intend to spend my life doing good works and improving the position of women in poor countries; I might start in Upper Burma. I also intend to learn to ride a bicycle, and drink Champagne."

"I need to know two things, Estelle," said Holmes. "And my friend and I guarantee that what you tell us will remain strictly between us. We will not divulge our secret to anyone, including Madame Tench."

"I love secrets," said Estelle dreamily. "I know lots and lots of them, but I hardly ever tell."

"My first question is about secrets. If you wanted to venture out of the Grange, to the village perhaps, without being detected, how would you go about it? Is there a secret passage?"

"The village is out-of-bounds," Estelle said primly, taking a long pull at her cigarette and stubbing the end out on the stone floor. "You'd be rusticated if you were caught."

"Let's assume, for the purposes of our discussion, that you do not intend to be caught."

She smiled. "There's a gate behind the tennis courts out to a small lane that leads to the village. The gate is padlocked, but the lock is rusted and it lifts off. You can't go to the village that

28

way though because the lane runs right by the door of the Wheatsheaf."

"A public house?"

"A den of iniquity," Estelle said firmly. "They serve the Devil's brew: whisky and strong waters." She turned again to me and shook a finger in my face. "You smell of whisky, Doctor holier-than-thou. You are going straight to hell."

"You could meet a friend in the lane?" asked Holmes.

Estelle smiled a slow smile. "A man?"

"A friend."

Angela pursed her lips. "You could. But you'd have to be quick. The only time would be during Promenade. We are not supervised during Promenade. We are supposed to act like ladies at Ascot: without the horses, and without the men."

"And the other question is one of letters, of correspondence. Madame Tench reads all your outgoing mail, I believe."

Estelle smiled again. "Madame Fishpot, the witch."

"I am sure that you have a method of circumventing her examination."

"Broderick, the gardener's son. He'll post a letter for the cost of the stamp and a penny on top. And he'll pick up letters to be called for, and parcels from the Post Office if they're double-wrapped. His name and address are on the outside and the lady's inside. That costs thruppence."

"And Eleanor used this service?"

"We all do, even though Broderick is a nasty little worm who peeks through keyholes, stinks of mould and begs for kisses."

"Thank you, Estelle," said Holmes, tipping his hat. "You have been very helpful."

Estelle leaned forward and whispered in his ear.

"Of course you may, my dear. Watson, give this young lady your cigarette packet."

She took the packet, winked at me and slipped it into her bosom.

Holmes and I walked through the Grange and across the front lawn. The police still assiduously probed the lake.

"We must visit the station, Watson. If Eleanor is not dead and she is not walking the halls of Aylescombe Grange in bloody bandages as a half-famished ghost, then she has left the town."

"Perhaps she took the mail coach."

He smiled. "Let us try the station first, and the mail coach if we fail there. We can examine the backdoor behind the tennis courts and perhaps pick up horses or a carriage at the Wheatsheaf."

We slipped behind the tennis courts and found a small wicket gate in the boundary wall of the Grange. A rusty padlock hung on the hasp of a lock, and it lifted off easily as Estelle had said.

"Note the numerous footprints, Watson. This is a busy thoroughfare."

He opened the gate, walked through and stopped. I saw that a dog cart stood in the lane just outside.

"Good evening, Mr Holmes," said the driver.

"Good evening, Mr Barker." Holmes climbed up beside Mr Barker and I sat in the back with Toby.

"Sergeant Callan has called in the West Surreys from the Stoughton Barracks to drag the lake," said Mr Barker. "To the station is it, gentlemen?"

He flicked his whip and we set off.

I kept silence for a few minutes, but I was burning with curiosity.

"Mr Barker spoke with Maggie, the plump girl at the lake, as we spoke to Estelle," Holmes said in response to my puzzled look. "Toby led him to her. Maggie gave him the information about the back door and the post that Estelle gave us."

"Cost half a crown, Doctor," said Mr Barker.

"It cost us an almost full packet of *Wild Woodbine* cigarettes," I replied.

The station master, an affable, red-faced chap as they invariably were, was happy to bring his staff together into the Gentlemen's Waiting Room to meet Holmes.

"The man we are looking for," Holmes said, "was possibly tall and in his fifties, with either grey mutton-chop whiskers or balding with a full grey moustache. He was with a girl, a striking young girl. Please pass the photograph around. She was not in Japanese clothes of course; I would imagine that she was in ordinary travelling dress."

The staff looked at the photograph, shook their heads and passed the picture on. Holmes frowned. "Wait, the young man with the cap, yes, you, sir."

A young man in a porter's uniform stepped forward nervously and saluted.

"Williams," said the station master. "Initial 'P' for Peter."

"Mr Williams," said Holmes softly. "You looked at the photograph, you made to pass it on, but you stopped and you looked again."

The young man looked at his toes. "I thought that the young lady was pretty, sir."

The station master and the other porters chuckled.

Holmes narrowed his eyes. "And."

The young man coloured. "A young lady looking like her took the first train to London the day before yesterday, sir. I noticed her because that train is mostly for locals who work in London: gentlemen and such."

"And because of her trim ankles, I make no doubt," said the station master, earning himself a cold look from Holmes.

"She wasn't with no man, though," Williams continued. "She was with an older lady."

"Describe," Holmes ordered.

"In her sixties, with grey hair in a bun behind; she was short, the girl was much taller. The lady was well-dressed, grey and with a flowery hat and a jolly smile. They both was all of a giggle, like."

Holmes turned to the station master. "Are there any trains from London earlier in the morning than the train to London that the ladies took?"

"No, sir."

"Very well. Any remarks, Mr Barker?"

"No, Mr Holmes, except to say that the plot thickens."

"Ha! Give Mr Williams, initial 'P', a shilling, Watson. He has been of material assistance."

We clambered back aboard the dog cart and set off for the town.

"If that young lady was indeed Eleanor," said Holmes, "she must have escaped from the school at dawn or before. She joined the older lady and travelled with her to London. From the station master's testimony, the lady could not have arrived in Guildford by train earlier that morning. It is a fair assumption that she came at least the day before, and she stayed the night at an hotel."

"Perhaps she took *The New Times* coach," I interjected.

Holmes smiled at Mr Barker. "What Guildford hotels would be suitable for a well-dressed lady, travelling alone?"

"The Angel and the White Hart. There may be others."

"We must spread ourselves. Watson and I to the Angel to pick up what information we may. If you would tackle the

White Hart, Mr Barker? Let us meet in the bar of the Angel in forty minutes for a council of war."

Mr Barker strode into the bar of the Angel and joined Holmes and I at our usual table in the window alcove. He grinned. "It is the Hart, gentlemen. A lady arrived in Guildford by train on Thursday afternoon. She had telegraphed a reservation from London and asked to be picked up at the station. The telegram was sent from the post office in the High Road, Balham. The lady offered her name as Mrs Phillips. She gave no indication of her reason for visiting Guildford, but she was in a jolly mood. She asked the violin trio that entertained guests after dinner to play Gilbert and Sullivan airs, especially those from —"

"*The Mikado*." Holmes smiled. "We are close, Mr Barker. We are, as children say, getting warm."

I blinked at him as two gentlemen appeared at the door of the bar. I immediately recognised Mr Percival and Mr August Lavery. They glared at each other, then at us and strode across the room towards our table.

Mr Barker stood. "I'll take my man in the Smoking Room," he murmured. He met Mr August Lavery halfway across the room and steered him out of the door.

Mr Percival Lavery stopped in front of our table and stared down over his nose at Holmes and I. "Which of you is the detective fellow?"

"I am Mr Sherlock Holmes. I understand that you are Percival Lavery."

Lavery frowned. "Well, man? Is it true that the girl drowned herself as I hear from the coppers? I'll need official confirmation before I can make my preparations."

"For the courts — the settlement?"

33

"Naturally." Mr Lavery sat, as Holmes stood. "I must inform you, sir that I no longer act on your behalf; no fees will be charged. Good day."

I stood and followed Holmes out of the door and into the lobby, leaving Mr Lavery sitting at the table gaping at us.

Barker joined us by the centre table. "I resigned from Mr August Lavery's employ, gentlemen. He is not taking it well."

"Good man," I said.

Percival Lavery strode past us, pale with anger. He ignored Holmes and I and marched into the Smoking Room, slamming the door behind him. Loud sounds of contention were instantly audible.

"Holmes, did you say that the older lady's name was Phillips?" I asked. "Was not that the name of the firm that installed the telephonic equipment at Aylescombe Grange? There was a plate on the side of the apparatus opposite my chair. It read 'Phillips of Balham'."

Holmes gave me a long look. "You see, Mr Barker? When it comes to synthesising ideas, very few men can beat my good friend, Doctor Watson."

I blushed and mumbled something deprecating.

"Carlisle?" Holmes asked Mr Barker.

He considered. "The local lads might have their noses put out of joint, sir. I'd say Dumfries. Ah, here is the man we need."

Sergeant Callan walked into the hotel looking haggard and care-worn. He came up to us massaging his back. "Two hours in a punt, and nothing to show, gentlemen. And the cook has lost an apple pie."

"We must ask you to send a telegram, Sergeant," Holmes said with a grin.

Holmes and I retreated to our rooms to wash and prepare for dinner. I made what notes on the case that I could, but I had to admit that I was in a state of confusion. Both Holmes and Mr Barker seemed to accept that the case had been solved by my observation regarding the telephonic apparatus, but I had not the faintest notion what part the telephone played in the matter. I was hesitant to admit my ignorance, however, and I kept my counsel.

"Do we dress for dinner Holmes?"

"In a hotel in Guildford? I hardly think so."

"It is the county seat."

"Fuss and feathers, Watson," said Holmes smoothing his frock coat. "Let us go down."

We entered the bar downstairs and found it packed with gentlemen in evening dress.

"I say, Holmes," I said, instantly feeling that we were the object of disdainful glances and whispered remarks. "Should we not return to our rooms and change into evening attire?"

"Never mind, gentlemen," said Mr Barker appearing by our side. He wore, like us, a plain black frockcoat. "These gentlemen are members of the Amateur Mendicant Society. I understand that their club premises in London are being renovated. They have engaged a private room upstairs. They are select, of course, and they have a strict code of dress. Nothing but the best for the AMS. This way to the dining room, gentlemen, I booked a table, and Sergeant Callan has news."

We dined very well on pea soup, a roast, and pears in brandy sauce. Callan kept his news to himself until we lit our cigars.

"Well, gentlemen," he said leaning back in his chair. "I have called off the West Surrey Regiment and given up the drag of the lake. I received this from my colleague in the Dumfries constabulary just before we sat down to dinner. He read the telegram. "Party in question at the hotel. Booked to Carlyle in the morning and on train arriving Euston at six-fifteen. Midland Grand Hotel overnight."

"Excellent," said Holmes. He turned to Mr Barker and held up a coin.

"Tails, Mr Holmes."

Holmes spun the coin, clapped it between his palms and showed it to me.

"Heads," I said.

"Watson and I take the train to London in the morning then. We must be at Euston Station to meet the Carlisle train."

I suppose my face fell.

"I'm sorry about your mail coach, old chap," said Holmes insincerely. "We will take it the next time we are called to Guildford."

I sighed, and both Mr Barker and Sergeant Callan gave Holmes reproachful looks.

Holmes frowned. "Oh, very well, I suppose as Watson broke open the case, we owe him his mail coach. Our quarry will overnight at the Midland Grand Hotel before proceeding south. We can catch them there."

The *New Times* mail coach clattered along Piccadilly in fine style as ladies in carriages waved and gentlemen on the pavement took off their hats to us, and we turned in to the stables at three minutes to seven precisely. I clambered down from the box, a little cramped, but exhilarated by the ride even beyond my high expectations. The countryside had been superb, alive with spring flowers, and the passage through the towns and London had been full of interest. I rescued Holmes from the inside of the coach, which he and another inside smoker had filled with a thick fug of tobacco smoke.

Holmes introduced me to his companion, a pale, lightly-built man who described himself as a builder. Arrangements were made for him to visit us the following day in Baker Street.

"Did you enjoy the journey?" I asked Holmes.

"Immensely," he answered to my surprise.

"Your fellow passenger was agreeable?"

"He was the lodger in the Sanderson case — the double murder — who was acquitted on a technicality. The case turned on a matter of identity. He condescended to tell me how he did it; it was an ingenious murder. I have invited him to tea tomorrow to go over the details."

Holmes and I caught a cab to the Midland Grand Hotel. I was most impressed by the decoration of the lobby, which was in the same romantic-medieval mood as the exterior. The main feature was an astonishingly dramatic staircase reaching almost to the full height of the building. There were passenger lifts, too, 'ascending chambers' as I remembered the novelties were known in their early days. A pageboy showed us to the sixth floor and the target suite. I dismissed him with thruppence tip, and Holmes knocked on the door.

After a long pause, the door opened an inch, and a man looked through the crack at us.

"May I speak with Mrs Phillips?" Holmes asked

"Who are you and what do you want with my wife?"

"Oh, David," said a soft voice from within the room. "That is the first time I have been addressed as 'Mrs Phillips' and the first time you have called me your wife!"

The man smiled, stepped back and opened the door. I saw that he held a horse whip in his right hand. A young, extremely-beautiful lady lay on a couch in the sitting room of the suite. I recognised her instantly as Eleanor, the missing girl. She wore a Japanese-style tea gown in bright silk, and she looked radiant.

"My name is Sherlock Holmes, and this is my friend Doctor Watson. We know everything."

Mrs Phillips leaned back with a languid yawn. "How tiresome for you."

Holmes turned to the young man. "You are Mr Phillips of Balham in London. You are a telephonic engineer. You met Eleanor Lavery at her school when you fitted an apparatus there six months ago."

The young man looked at his wife, and then smiled back at us, "That is so. I suppose I've been expecting somebody. You mayn't part us, you know; we are man and wife.

"I assure you we have no intention of attempting to do so."

"Very well." Mr Phillips ushered us to plush chairs opposite the sofa.

Holmes folded himself into his seat while I sat primly on the edge of mine.

"We fell for each other immediately," said Mr Phillips. "Eleanor sent a note to my office —"

"Good Lord," I spluttered. I could not believe that a young lady of good breeding had initiated a correspondence with a strange man. It was unheard of, and dishonourable of the man to receive it.

Holmes winked at me. "Go on, Mr Phillips."

"I therefore made it my business to see to the calibration and maintenance of the telephonic equipment at the Grange myself. Eleanor and I met privately in the School grounds at least every week, and eventually, after an appropriate interval, we made our vows. You must understand that I did not want to proceed in an underhand fashion, but Eleanor intimated that her headmistress would instantly ban me from the premises if our attraction to each other were made public, and that her step-father was intent on keeping her from the company of men — even suitable men of her class and station in life. Her uncle had

38

made certain advances to her, the blaggard, but Eleanor would not countenance me giving him a thrashing. I carry a horsewhip in the hope that he will appear on our doorstep.

"Our meetings were clandestine, but they were all perfectly seemly, sirs; one of the other girls was always present. I am a working man and therefore might justifiably be considered an unsuitable husband for Eleanor, but I have formed my own business venture with a little capital I borrowed from a relation, and I now employ three men and a boy. I count the Bishop of Ely and Mr Gilbert, the librettist, as clients. I am in no way dependant on my wife's inheritance. Telephony is the coming thing, gentlemen; I can hardly keep up with demand."

I clasped the boy's hand and shook it. "You should thank the German Emperor's horse," I suggested.

Mr Phillips gave me an odd look.

"Who was your chaperone?" Holmes asked.

"I'm not sure of her name, sir, but she was a well-built young lady." He turned to Eleanor.

"She won't get into trouble, will she?" Eleanor asked softly.

"Not for chaperoning your meetings, no," Holmes replied.

"Then it was Maggie."

"So I expected. She is a close friend, Madame?"

"We were practically inseparable." Eleanor turned to her husband. "Mr Holmes called me Madame, David. Isn't he a sweetie?"

"Terribly sweet, my love." They kissed.

Holmes paled, and I coughed to hide a slight chuckle.

"Why did you not convey your bride-to-be to Scotland yourself?" I asked Mr Phillips when he had disengaged from his wife. "It is the usual thing is it not — with the girl's relatives in hot pursuit?"

"You are out-of-date, sir; if I may correct you. Under the new law, one of the couple who wish to marry must have resided in Scotland for at least three weeks. I took the train to Dumfries and spent three dull weeks there to establish my eligibility to marry. I procured a certificate from the hotel manager, and made my way to Greta Green to meet my future wife. Eleanor was perfectly safe; she travelled up with my mother. We were married by the blacksmith in Gretna, in the traditional style, over the anvil."

He exchanged a fond look with his wife. "We will spend our honeymoon in Lyme Regis, by the sea."

We wished the happy couple the very best of luck, and set off downstairs to the hotel telegraph office.

"I do not envy Barker his onerous task, Watson," Holmes said as we took the lift down to the lobby. "He called the coin wrong. He must inform the brothers Lavery that Eleanor is out of their power, and legally married. Mr Percival Lavery, our client, thought that his niece was safely locked away at school until her majority in a year's time. Uncle August thought that he had time to press his case. The brothers did not factor the telephonic engineer and Gretna Green into their nefarious plans."

"One thing —"

"Margaret, of course. She missed her friend, was jealous and wanted attention: thus the clothes in the lake, the missing food (obviously), the bloody knife and Ophelia's flowers. She wore some of Eleanor's clothes, and thus fooled Toby. He sang in a strangled squawk.

"Modesty at marriage-tide
Well becomes a pretty bride!

Estelle gave us multiple clues. I sometimes wonder — this is for your private ear, my friend — whether more is going on in the brains of some persons of the female species than is obvious from the outside. Look at Madame Neruda, Miss Nightingale, and the late Lady Sarah Davies."

"And the Woman, Holmes: Miss Adler."

He nodded. "But then we think of Mrs Weldon, the bane of mad doctors, and the frothy damsels coming out each Season, and we must shake our heads in utter confusion. Who can plumb the feminine mind?"

Holmes checked his watch. "We did not collect a fee for this case, my friend, and we have had to absorb costs." He gave me a sly look. "Including certain extraordinary travel expenses. Nevertheless, I call the Aylescombe affair a success and suggest that we treat ourselves to a roast at Simpson's. What do you say?"

"An excellent idea."

We caught a cab outside the hotel and set off for the Strand.

"I thought of Gretna at eleven forty-three yesterday morning," said Holmes. "I made a note on my shirt cuff — see. I must check when Barker had his first notion. He did well, I thought, for a neophyte."

I considered. "Should we get a telephone apparatus, Holmes? Mr Phillips calls telephony the coming thing, and according to the papers, the machines are popular in America."

"No, no. Conditions obtain in America that require the use of such instruments. In London we have a superabundance of postal deliveries, messengers, telegraph offices and errand boys. The absence of servants has compelled America to adopt telephonic systems for domestic purposes. The telephone will never catch on in Britain. That, I may absolutely guarantee."

###

Murder at the Savoy

"Wake up, Holmes," I whispered over the hubbub of the audience as the electric lights were lit and people stood, stretched and exchanged remarks. I gave my friend a sharp nudge in the ribs and he blinked awake, yawned and looked around the auditorium of the Savoy Theatre.

"Is it over?"

"No, this is the interval." I waved an indulgence slip. "Thirty minutes, according to this note. It's an extended interval as the set-up of the ghost scene is complex."

Holmes yawned again, squinted at the bright lights and hummed an air from the *Mikado*.

"What do you think of it so far?" I asked.

"Sir Despard Murgatroyd, the lead, exclaims that he is moody and sad in a baritone consistently one-sixteenth of a tone flat. The alleged soprano who plays Rose sings in a strangled squawk, and Robin Oakapple, the virtuous farmer, is either drunk or experiencing a concatenation of mental aberrations."

"Yes, Mr Grossmith seems to be more than usually incapacitated by first-night nerves," I agreed. "And I must say the choice of name for the opera is perverse: *Ruddygore*. It is on the edge of poor taste." I lowered my voice. "Between ourselves, I'd say it's not a patch on *The Mikado*."

Holmes pulled out his watch, checked the time and smiled. "The Criterion Grill is but a brisk walk away. What do you say to a roast and a bottle of the house red? It is a very drinkable Bordeaux."

"But, my dear fellow, we are here at the invitation of Mr D'Oyly Carte. We can't just waltz off leaving two empty seats three rows from the front of the stalls. It would be ungrateful and rude."

Holmes smiled a devilish smile. "The Criterion does excellent roast beef, thin-sliced at the table, for a mere half-crown."

I held up my hand in melodramatic horror. "Get thee behind me, Holmes!"

He sighed. "Very well, Watson. I see that you are a slave to duty. I —"

The noise of the crowd suddenly swelled and several people pointed up to a man in a box above us. Some men in the audience jeered and shook their fists at him.

"I say, Holmes," I said looking up. "That is Lord Randolph Churchill. He resigned from the government a couple of months ago."

The jeering grew louder. Lord Randolph stood and glowered down at the audience over his thick walrus moustache. His wife, the society beauty Jenny Churchill, stood beside him, looking pale, but defiant.

Holmes writhed up from his seat and faced the audience. "No politics!" he shouted at the top of his voice.

There was a shocked silence, and then the usual theatre crowd hubbub was renewed. Lord Randolph bowed stiffly to Holmes, and Holmes returned the gesture. He turned back to me. "Not all mobs are spawned in Whitechapel, Watson. You may find them in Park Lane as well as the Commercial Road, and particularly at the Palace of Westminster. Six months ago, the same people who cried out against Lord Randolph now would have cheered him to the Upper Circle."

I stopped a pageboy and passed him the stub for the interval drinks I had ordered. I held up sixpence and his eyes glittered. "Five minutes; after that you lose a penny a minute. Clear?"

He had already disappeared into the crowd; he was immediately replaced by another page. "Mr Carte's compliments, gentlemen, and would Mr Holmes and Doctor Watson care to join him in his office for refreshment?"

The boy led us up a set of back stairs and along a corridor hung with paintings of characters from the plays of Gilbert and Sullivan. He knocked at a fine oaken door and ushered us in to Mr Carte's office. Mr Carte and several other gentlemen were clustered in front of the fireplace of his well-appointed office drinking Champagne. I recognised Lord Randolph and several other politicians from both sides of the aisle.

Mr Carte stepped from the group and held out his hand as Holmes made the introductions with the polite assurance he invariably displayed in social situations that involved people he classed as having merit: men of substance rather than mere rank.

Mr Carte was, as always, perfectly groomed and dressed and his trim beard, moustache and neat hair framed a handsome face. I knew him to be a skilled theatrical and musical agent who had acted for Monsieur Gounod and Herr Offenbach, and now listed Madame Clara Schumann and Mr Oscar Wilde among his clients — together with Messrs Gilbert and Sullivan, of course.

He introduced us to Sir Rutgar Montague, a bald and very corpulent gentleman, and he in turn introduced Lord Randolph.

"I know Mr Holmes by reputation of course," said Lord Randolph, bowing politely.

Mr Carte called for more Champagne and continued his description of the telephonic apparatus that had been installed in his office in permanent connection with an identical device in the home of Mr Gilbert. He explained that Mr Gilbert required each day's takings to be rendered into code and transmitted to him the following morning. He would then calculate his royalty as a percentage of that sum, less expenses. Lord Randolph and

Holmes drifted away and murmured together by the fireplace as Sir Rutgar buttonholed me. I took note of the baronet's flushed complexion, yellowish jowls and his squinting, red-rimmed eyes and I sighed. I realized that I was in danger of being dragooned into an impromptu consultation with the portly gentleman as to the state of his liver and his no doubt many and multifarious ailments.

"I am afraid that Sir Arthur will not join us, gentlemen," said Mr Carte. "He is ministering to Miss Braham who is not quite herself this evening. Mr Gilbert is in his usual cubbyhole up in the gods, keeping an eye on us mortals from Olympus."

"Is there anything that I can do?" I offered.

"No. Mr Gilbert is less than sociable at the best of times, and on an opening night — oh, you mean Miss Braham, our wilting Rose."

Carte considered. "I hardly like to take advantage of your kind offer, Doctor, but there is a matter in which you might help us, and with advantage to yourself as far as the quality of the second act of the play is concerned. Mr Grossmith is consumed with nerves — that is perfectly usual on first nights, of course, but I have not seen the poor man in quite such a tizzy before."

"I would be happy to help, if I can."

I took my leave of Sir Rutgar and he gave me a cold look in return. I left Mr Carte's office and a servant ushered me downstairs through narrow passageways, all lit by glowing electric globes, to Mr Grossmith's dressing room. A call boy sat on a chair outside the door.

"Is Mr Grossmith available?" the servant asked him.

"Who's asking?"

"I am a doctor," I answered. "Mr Carte has requested that I visit Mr Grossmith."

The boy stood and rapped on the door. "Mr Carte sent a doctor, sir. Are you in?"

Silence.

The boy held up his hand. "Give him a mo."

A short man in evening dress bustled past us as I heard a faint, choked cry from behind Mr Grossmith's door. "*Non è possibile.*"

The boy shook his head. "Sorry, Doctor, Mr G is not at home to callers tonight."

The short man stopped and turned, and I recognised Sir Arthur Sullivan, the composer and conductor of the operetta. "Are you a doctor, sir?"

I bowed. "Doctor John Watson at your service, Sir Arthur."

He returned my bow. "I should deem it a personal favour, Doctor Watson, if you would examine one of our young ladies, Miss Braham. She is not at all herself this evening. I fear that some malady has taken hold of the poor girl and flown to her throat."

I immediately agreed, and Sir Arthur wrung my hand and led the way to Miss Braham's dressing room.

I met Holmes at the entrance to the auditorium.

"How is Mr Grossmith?" he asked.

"*Non a casa,*" I replied. "His dressing room door was stoutly defended."

"Oh, dear." Holmes grinned a jaguar grin. "There is always the Criterion Grill."

"Avaunt thee, Holmes! I was asked by Sir Arthur to attend Miss Braham."

He raised his eyebrows.

"*Enceinte*; I should say four or five months gone. Her costume was far too tight. I prescribed letting it out an inch or two each month until she comes to term."

"Ah, that explains her strangled high notes."

I gave him a quizzical look.

"She is singing for two."

A pageboy stood by the end seat of our row holding a tray. I recognised him, with a pang of guilt, as the boy I had sent to collect our interval drinks. Holmes consulted his watch. "You are twenty-two minutes late."

The boy flushed an angry red and handed us each a glass of warm red wine.

"Give him a florin, Watson. He shows an admirable reverence for duty."

The pageboy sighed. "Mr Carte's orders, sir, and we're not allowed to accept tips (when the lights are up and he can see us anyway)."

The house lights dimmed on cue, and Holmes winked. "The two-bob is not a tip, it is a waiting charge, as with a hansom cab."

The boy frowned, shrugged, slipped the coin into his pocket and disappeared as the orchestra struck up the introduction to Act Two of *Ruddygore*.

"Holmes, Holmes." I shook his shoulders and he blinked awake.

"Mr Carte desires my presence on a matter of urgency."

Holmes winced as Miss Braham, as Rose, sang to her sailor lover.

> *"My hopes will be blighted, I fear, my dear;*
> *In a month you'll be going to sea, quite free,*
> *And all of my wishes, you'll throw to the fishes*
> *As though they were never to be; poor me!*

We met Carte in the corridor outside one of the exits talking with a page.

"Where?" he asked the boy softly.

"Second row of the Balcony, third from the end, 62, sir. We draped him with the cloth and laid him out on the sofa by the men's lavatory. His niece is with him, very upset."

"Retiring room, not lavatory, Bates," said Mr Carte coldly. "You are not at a music hall."

"Can I be of assistance?" I asked.

"Ah Doctor, and Mr Holmes," said Mr Carte. "A member of the audience has been taken ill (in a seat on the Balcony and not the Stalls, thank goodness)."

He frowned. "But I fear that I have already trespassed upon your good nature, Doctor, I am reluctant —"

"Oh, don't worry about Watson, Mr Carte," said Holmes, clapping me on the back in his annoying way. "He is never happier than when he is working on the nearly dead. I had to drag him away from his practice for today's glorious entertainment. There is nothing he would rather do than view your patient. I will second him."

We followed the pageboy and Mr Carte upstairs and along a richly decorated corridor to where a large man in evening dress lay across a sofa being ministered to by a pair of young ladies and a young gentleman. I recognised, with another pang of conscience, that the sick man was Sir Rutgar Montague, Bart.

A young lady ceased flapping a frilly handkerchief in Sir Rutgar's face and turned to me with a fierce expression. "You are Doctor Watson?"

I admitted my identity and accepted a scolding from the lady as she recounted that her uncle had mentioned my previous reluctance to discuss his ailments. Here, the young lady contended, was the result of my neglect.

I moved her gently aside and examined Sir Rutgar. He was barely conscious. The ruddy complexion I had noticed was gone and he was pale and breathing in a shallow, halting fashion. There was a slight froth about his lips. I loosened his collar.

"What did he last eat?" I asked.

"We dined at the Criterion Grill," said the young lady, the baronet's niece, in a stiff tone. "The roast."

I heard Holmes cough.

I took the gentleman's temperature — high — and felt his pulse — thready and uneven — and mopped his brow with a damp towel. He stirred, and seemed to rally. He called for wine, for which I substituted brandy from Mr Carte's stock.

Several groups of ladies and gentlemen passed us on their way to the exit. I saw another troubled frown flicker across Mr Carte's brow as one gentleman, obviously in a state of inebriation, waved his programme and cried "Take this rubbish off and give us the *Mikado*."

Sir Rutgar heaved himself into a sitting position, batted away his female relatives and rebuttoned his collar as the page arrived with a large brandy. "Thankee. Just a slight bilious indisposition; often happens when I overindulge. Too much bread-and butter pudding at the Criterion. Capital meal, though."

Holmes gave me an accusing look.

More members of the audience passed us, even though we could hear through the auditorium doors that the operetta was still in full flow.

"It's raining outside," Holmes said gently. "People are afraid they won't get cabs."

Mr Carte shook his head and blinked at him. "If Gilbert doesn't get at least three curtain calls, there will be more than thunder storms."

The following day, Holmes appeared from his bedroom, wiping his hands on a towel as Mrs Hudson and Billy brought in breakfast. We ate and then settled ourselves by the fire with our after-breakfast pipes and the newspapers.

"Look at this Holmes, 'Another Brilliant Success'. Poppycock, I'm afraid. The play was neither engaging nor well done."

Holmes flicked down a corner of his *Sunday Times* and gave me a quizzical look.

"The *Sunday Express* on *Ruddygore*."

Holmes sniffed. "According to the *Sunday Times*, the operetta was 'received with every demonstration of delight by a distinguished and representative audience'. Ha! They write only of the first act. The Sunday music and theatrical critics have to meet deadlines for their copy, and the play ran late. They slipped out well before the end and they commented on the first part only. The critics of the piece have vented their indignation at the title and the second half."

I thought that an unlikely explanation, but, as I had no other I did not venture another comment.

My eye caught an item in the stop press. "My goodness, Holmes, the gentleman who was taken ill at the Savoy, the baronet, died early this morning. No cause of death has been ascertained."

Holmes snapped his paper and turned the page. "There are ominous stirrings in the Maupertuis case. I shall have to return to the continent."

That hung between us for a while, as I had advised Holmes, as his physician as well as his friend, to refrain from further exertions in that convoluted fraud until he had fully recovered his health and renewed his mental faculties. He had, in my opinion, over-stretched even his great intellect in his pursuit across Europe of the foul Baron Maupertuis; a period of quiet recuperation was absolutely necessary.

"I looked up baronet in your index, Holmes," I said, changing the subject. "Did you know —"

"That they are not members of the Peerage? Yes. They are commoners, sirs by courtesy, not right."

"I was about to say that," I said in a cold tone. I returned to my newspaper, and we maintained a sullen silence between us for the rest of the morning.

***

One of the equinoctial gales of late September shook our window glass and whistled down the chimney as I entered the sitting room. I greeted Holmes and looked out of the window. Clouds scudded across the sky, and below our windows in Baker Street a bareheaded telegraph boy struggled against the wind on his bicycle, his hair blown back and his eyes red-rimmed.

Mrs Hudson had laid out a fine kedgeree for breakfast and I helped myself to that and to what coffee was left after Holmes' avid attentions. He sat back in his chair, arms around his knees, smoking his churchwarden pipe. I thought to open the window a sliver as the room was already a fug of tobacco smoke, but I saw an article in my newspaper that stopped me.

"Holmes, there has been another incident at the Savoy Theatre; it is just like the one earlier in the year — in January wasn't it? A gentleman was taken ill during Sunday's performance of *Ruddigore* (I see that they have improved the title). I say, it is the first victim's brother! Sir Redvers Montague was resident in Dublin, but returned from Ireland in January for his brother's funeral and to take up his duties as baronet of Montague Manor in Cheshire. And now he is taken ill in the same theatre at a production of the same opera. It is extraordinary."

"Coincidences always are."

"But Holmes, consider the subject matter of the operetta! It concerns several bad baronets who —"

The doorbell rang downstairs, there was a heavy tread on the stairs and the door opened.

"Mr D'Oyly Carte," Billy announced.

I jumped up and shook Mr Carte's hand. "Mr Carte, pray take a seat," said Holmes, waving his pipe stem at the sofa in his casual manner.

Mr Carte sat on our sofa and crossed his legs. I offered him coffee and my cigar case, but he declined.

"Mr Holmes and Doctor Watson, I am at a stand. You were witnesses to the disagreeable incident that occurred on the Balcony on our opening night in January. Then on Sunday we had a precisely identical occurrence." He sighed and shook his head. "Only this time in the Stalls, seat 47, third row back and at the dramatic climax of the opera."

"The victim was Sir Rutgar's brother, Sir Redvers Montague, newly established baronet of Montague Manor," I added.

Mr Carte nodded. "Sir Rutgar suffered the bilious attack that killed him in seat 62 of the Balcony: third row back, three seats in. Sir Redvers was taken ill in the Stalls, third row back, three seats in. Word is spreading around our rival houses as these things invariably do. We will not fill those two seats, and we have trouble with any seat in a similar position. It looks worse as we are playing to full houses after our dreadful, scorching summer; the seats will be like missing teeth and the subject of speculation and anxiety." He ran his finger around the inside of his collar, as if he were too warm on what was a very cold day.

"Are you sure that you won't take some refreshment, Mr Carte," I asked solicitously.

"Thank you, perhaps coffee if that might be managed without inconvenience."

I called down to Billy for a fresh pot and resumed my seat by the fireplace.

"Under no circumstances," Mr Carte continued, "must the Savoy get a reputation as a jinxed house. Our clientele were troubled when we installed the electric light. I went onstage and broke an electric bulb to convince sceptics that the new lighting is safer than gas."

"I thought the lighting superb," I said. "I remarked to Holmes that —"

"Actors are the most superstitious of mortals," Mr Carte continued in an emotional tone. "If we have another incident, I will not answer for the cast and crew, let alone our patrons. By the nature of what we purvey — theatrical entertainment — we expect our audiences to engage their imaginations. Between ourselves, gentlemen, a theatre audience is little more than a genteel mob ready to run amok at the slightest provocation."

He pulled a handkerchief from his pocket and mopped his brow. "It did not help that Mr Grossmith was taken ill, more ill than is usual, at the start of the run, and that Miss Braham was not quite herself and had to leave the company in May."

Mr Carte gave me a pointed look, but I said nothing. I felt no pangs of remorse that I did not inform him of Miss Braham's pregnancy. It was a question of doctor and client privilege. However, I avoided his eye and I was relieved when the door opened and Mrs Hudson bustled in with coffee and with biscotti from the Italian coffee shop by the station.

I handed coffee as Mrs Hudson withdrew and I pressed Mr Carte to try the biscotti.

"Thank you, Doctor, but no. I breakfasted very amply with Mr Gilbert. The inner man is replete, but my nervous system is in tatters. You have breakfasted with Mr Gilbert? It is not a practice that I would recommend, even to persons of iron constitution. He has an opinion, a vehement opinion, on most matters; on subjects that affect him more nearly — matters of finance mostly — he is fierce indeed."

He considered. "We are men of the world, gentlemen. I conceive that I may be frank. The partnership between Mr Sullivan and Mr Gilbert (or the other way around, depending on which of them I am with) is fragile. Indeed it has shattered and been clumsily repaired by Helen Lenoir (my assistant) and myself on numerous occasions."

He stirred his coffee, and smiled. "The *succès fou* of *The Mikado* healed what I thought might be the final breach between my sensitive composer and my brittle and litigious librettist, but now we have *Ruddigore*."

He shrugged and his voice took on a darker tone. "The play suffers in comparison with the previous production. *The Mikado* is a hard act to follow. And changing the name of our current play from *Ruddygore* to *Ruddigore* has upset the more superstitious members of the cast, and upset Mr Gilbert, who is entirely, utterly and vociferously without the slightest trace of superstition. A reporter told Gilbert that ruddy meant bloody and was therefore unacceptable in a Christian theatre. He answered to the contrary. He said, in that case, if he said that he admired the fellow's ruddy countenance, which he did, he would be saying that he liked his bloody cheek, which he didn't."

Holmes and Mr Carte laughed aloud. I held my tongue, for I thought the comment in poor taste, and I entirely disagreed with Mr Gilbert on the propriety of the original name of the opera.

The doorbell rang, and a moment later Billy arrived at the door and presented Holmes with a telegram. He passed it to me, and after craving Mr Carte's indulgence, I read it.

"The telegram is from Inspector Gregson of Scotland Yard; he is investigating the cases we have been discussing. He regrets to inform Mr Holmes that Sir Redvers, the younger brother of Sir Rutgar Montague (deceased), has died. He expired at nine this morning at the family's London home in Kensington. The inspector would like to meet Mr Holmes to discuss the case."

"Well, that's that," said Mr Carte, rising from his seat. "*Ruddigore* will come off as soon as we can replace it. A revival of *Pirates of Penzance*, I think. Yes, we could get by with *Pirates*."

I stood with him. "I understand from the articles in the newspapers that there is no evidence of any foul play at the Savoy, Mr Carte. You may take some comfort from that."

"A coincidence then?" he answered gravely. "That would be worse news. I would laugh in the face of any playwright who came to me with a melodrama that had two brothers, baronets, taken mortally ill during a production of *Ruddigore*, a play about bad baronets."

He turned to Holmes. "I see that the police are keeping you informed on developments in the case, or cases rather. Might I therefore implore you to take a more direct interest on my behalf, on the behalf of the Savoy?"

Holmes stood and held out his hand. "I should count it a privilege, Mr Carte."

I ushered Mr Carte to his carriage, and returned upstairs to find Holmes bustling about his desk and Billy standing at the door.

"It's absolutely icy outside Holmes," I said. "And blowing like the Great Simoom."

Holmes turned to Billy. "The remaining newspapers may be put in the box room, Billy, if there's space."

"The general will get them," said Billy, shaking his head. "He's on the rampage again." He bundled the week's newspapers into his arms and pounded upstairs.

"Something will have to be done," I suggested.

"About Billy, or the rat?" Holmes rummaged through the drawers of his desk. "Where are the telegraph forms? Mrs Hudson's constant tidying up causes havoc with my indexing system. The forms should be precisely —"

I extracted a form from a neat pile on my desktop and waved it at him.

"Very well. And perhaps you may recall the address of the county coroner? You spoke to me of him in connection with the missing American boy in the summer."

"His office is at St Lawrence, Pountney Hill, EC."

I smiled at a recollection. "He is a rather droll person, Holmes. He suggested that we could take a cab, or arrive more quickly at the Mortuary by stepping in front of an omnibus."

Holmes turned and frowned, and I meekly took dictation.

We met Inspector Gregson at the Coroner's office at St Laurence where he sat drinking tea in front of the Coroner's desk. I had always thought him one of the brightest of the Scotland Yard men; not quite as dogged as Lestrade, but less reliant on his nose and more likely to use his brain. He sat, sniffing and nursing a cold.

The Coroner, who I had first met in the summer, was the very affable Mr Purchase. I saw that, as on the previous occasion that I had been in his office, a large alabaster Phrenological head marked with coloured lines and strange symbols stood on his desk, this time next to two files.

Mr Purchase stood and shook my hand. "Doctor Watson, how good to see you again," he said with a trace of Welsh in his accent.

"And an honour, of course, to meet the famous Mr Sherlock Holmes. The general public are not aware of your great reputation, but I can assure you that in mortuary circles your name resounds in a clear, strong peal of professional appreciation."

Holmes bowed, and he could not conceal a glitter in his eyes and something close to a self-satisfied smirk. He looked up and Mr Purchase seemed to freeze as he stared at Holmes, particularly at his receding brow. Holmes regarded the Coroner with an amused frown.

"Ahem," I said.

"Oh, oh," said Mr Purchase, reddening. "How terribly rude of me, and on our first acquaintance too. I do apologise Mr Holmes. It is just that I have never seen a more prominent organ of causality and comparison than on your brow. That is the area of the skull associated in Phrenological studies with intellectual prowess, particularly deductive reasoning. I might have expected a pronounced, ah, um —" He looked at Holmes, Gregson and I, and patted the alabaster head. "All nonsense of course."

Mr Purchase opened his office door, called for more tea, sat behind his desk again and opened one of the folders. "The body of Sir Rutgar was returned to the Montague family for burial last January. But I had photographs made. Here they are."

He passed Holmes a sheaf of photographs. He examined each one, and passed it to me, and I to Gregson.

"He died from multiple organ failure — liver, spleen, kidneys and finally heart," said Mr Purchase. "I have seen worse in chronic alcoholics, but not much worse. He was dead within hours of what we assume was the onset of symptoms in the Savoy Theatre."

He indicated a photograph of the body face down.

"Sir Rutgar was a county squire, with, at one time, a love of country pursuits — shooting, riding to hounds and cricket. He had grown somewhat rotund, but the many wounds that he received on the hunting field were still upon him as scars, dozens, scores of them. And I must admit that I missed something, Mr Holmes. That is, in your terms, I saw but I did not properly observe."

Holmes smiled and nodded.

Mr Purchase pointed to a dot or puncture in the body's right buttock, just below the hip. It was clearly a recent wound, recent at the time the photograph had been taken, as the skin around the puncture was bright, as if slightly inflamed.

"Ice pick," I suggested. "Stiletto?"

"Here is another photograph to indicate the scale."

"Hypodermic," I corrected myself.

Mr Purchase slipped a sheet of paper from the file. "I requested that the police inspector in charge of the case question members of the family with regard to medicines the deceased might have been taking, particularly by injection. As you can see, the site of the injection in the lower back makes it unlikely that it was self-administered, and the slight brightness about the wound suggested that the injection might have been a violent one.

"According to police reports, Sir Rutgar was unmarried and he lived with his niece (his sister's daughter) at a villa in Norbury. I am informed that Sir Rutgar was in poor health and although afflicted with lung and liver problems, he took no medicine by injection. It is possible that he have been dosing himself with some quack remedy, but unlikely that he administered it by needle.

"In his unconscious state he was ministered to by a local physician who noted that the symptoms of the malady that killed him included very low blood pressure, nausea, seizures and hallucinations. He died when his liver, kidneys and spleen simply ceased operation."

"You suspected poison administered by injection?" I asked. "Perhaps self-administered?"

The Coroner smiled. "I am afraid that I did not. The pinprick was anomalous, but I could think of no known poison that would induce the symptoms described and kill so quickly."

He stood. "Let me show you something else." He led us out of his office along tiled passageways and downstairs to a set of double doors marked 'Mortuary' in green letters. I remembered them from a case earlier in the year. The temperature dropped as we passed through the doors into a large white-tiled room. Wall-mounted and hanging gas jets lit the room as brightly as a butcher's shop, and along one wall was a framework of polished wood in which rows of metal doors were set. A handwritten notice hung on one: 'Bodies Feet First If You Please'.

The penetrating odour of decay was far less obvious than on my visit in the spring when the weather had been unusually hot.

"It is very much cooler now than on my last visit," I remarked.

"Yes," said the coroner. "Our patent system of steam-driven fans blowing air over blocks of American ice is working well now that the weather is more cooperative."

A row of five dissecting tables occupied the centre of the room, all empty except for the first on which the body of a corpulent man lay face up. It bore a strong resemblance to Sir Rutgar Montague.

"This is Sir Redvers Montague, the brother of the gentleman who died in January," said Mr Purchase. "He was a retired stock broker before he inherited the title. Not a well man; he suffered from severe gout and was in very poor shape generally. Help me turn him over, would you, Doctor?"

I did so, and immediately noticed a livid mark on his otherwise unscarred back. "I say, Holmes, that is another injection mark."

Mr Purchase smiled. "It is no more than four inches from the location of the mark on the buttocks of the first corpse. And identical in all other respects, except that it is much more prominent as there are few other scars. Sir Redvers was also dead within hours of his seizure at the Savoy. The symptoms in this second case were identical to those of the first."

Holmes took out his magnifying glass. "May I?" He gave the corpse a thorough examination. "Interesting."

"The crust of white dust?" Mr Purchase suggested. "Indeed, there are minute traces of two white powders surrounding the wound, one more granular and crystalline than the other. There were similar traces at the wound site of Sir Rutgar."

"A downward thrust with a hypodermic needle," Holmes mused. "The victims were probably sitting."

"I have analysed the substances found in both wounds and they are identical," Mr Purchase said. "Chalk and sugar. Any other constituent, the fatal one we may presume if we accept the poisoning hypothesis, left no traces and did not react to the standard tests for the common domestic poisons like strychnine, arsenic and prussic acid. I have prepared samples that you might like to take with you, Mr Holmes, to check my findings. I must advise you to take very great care with the specimens, sir; something volatile killed the two gentlemen, and it may very well continue to be active even though it cannot be seen."

I was taken aback. Sugar and chalk? What could those innocuous substances have to do with the deaths of the two men?

Inspector Gregson blew his nose. "Could I ask a great favour of you, Mr Holmes? The two cases have been put together and given to me. I should deem it an honour were you to take an interest, sir."

"Certainly, Inspector Gregson. In fact, I should inform you that I have been engaged by Mr D'Oyly Carte to represent the interests of the Savoy in the matter. I shall be pleased to second your efforts. We might start at the theatre, which seems to be the main point of connection between the two deaths. And I suggest that you invite the family members of each baronet to return to the scene with us. The summons to the relatives of the victims would carry more weight if it came from an official source."

We made our slow way home as the cab horse had to trot directly into the icy wind and it shied frequently. The cabby asked permission to take a more roundabout, sheltered route and I gave it.

I was in a sombre mood, shocked that two persons, whether of the peerage or not, had died in such sudden and mysterious circumstances. Holmes was clearly too preoccupied planning his analysis of the substance in the samples given to him by Mr Purchase to engage in conversation.

We reached Baker Street and our cosy sitting room at last. I occupied myself with starting a new notebook on the case as Billy stoked the fire and muttered the latest situation reports on his battle with the rat that had taken up residence in our box room.

Holmes donned his old, chemical-stained and threadbare dressing gown, many times rescued from Mrs Hudson as she tried to persuade the rag and bone man to take it away. "The sample is tiny, Watson. We have chalk, and we have a few grains of sugar that were perhaps in solution with the substance that caused the deaths. I do not have a sufficient quantity to conduct many of the standard tests for poisons so I shall rely on

Mr Purchase's analysis for now. The symptoms exhibited by the baronets do not point to any agent that I have heard of."

"The speed of action of the agent is most remarkable."

Holmes nodded agreement. "Strychnine and prussic acid kill in minutes, but their symptoms are quite different from those presented by the baronets."

Holmes filled his churchwarden pipe with a new blend that I had from my tobacconist on trial. "I have to plan my strategy very carefully. I shall smoke a pipe or two, or perhaps three as I contemplate my dispositions."

Holmes lit his pipe and tucked his legs under him in his strange Oriental fashion and he was soon surrounded by a fug of tobacco smoke.

I sat at my desk and made a mental list of possible agents, or rather a list of poisons that I thought we could safely exclude from our suspicions. The symptoms that I had observed, and those reported by the victim's doctors to the police, seemed to rule out strychnine, arsenic, prussic acid and many of the poisons Holmes and I had encountered in previous cases. The rapidity with which death occurred suggested something of an order of magnitude more toxic than the common alkaloids. My thoughts inevitably veered towards the East and the fiendish substances that the Oriental mind seemed to delight in inventing.

Holmes finished his second pipe, tapped it out on the grate and reached for the Persian slipper in which he kept my tobacco; I checked my watch and reminded him of our appointment at the Savoy. He dressed, and we made our way by cab against strong winds and now through driving rain to the Strand. We alighted outside the main entrance of the Savoy Theatre and we were conducted to the dimly-lit auditorium where Mr Carte and Inspector Gregson awaited us.

"There have been no other reports of injuries or illness?" Holmes asked Mr Carte.

"No more than usual, and nothing fatal," Mr Carte answered.

Holmes turned to me. "Good, then you will be safe, my dear fellow."

I blinked nervously at him.

"Mr Carte, may I prevail upon you to instruct your electrical man to turn up the house lights to their fullest extent? I intend to examine the seats that the unfortunate brothers occupied."

"I may be able to do better than that, Mr Holmes," Mr Carte answered.

He went into the wings and returned with an electric globe on a long lead or cable. He lowered it over the back of seat 47 in the stalls and waved to his engineer. The globe sprang to life, blinding me for a moment. Holmes knelt behind the seat and closely examined it through his lens. He took out an envelope, scraped something from the upholstery and stood. He handed me the envelope. "Take care. Do not breathe the particles."

I gingerly took a peek inside. "A tiny amount of dust, no, white powder." I gave the envelope back to Holmes and he tucked it into his waistcoat pocket.

He nodded. "The other seat, Mr Carte?"

We followed Mr Carte as he carried the bright globe to the other side of the auditorium and up to the gallery. The length of the cable attached to the globe seemed to make no difference to its brightness. I wondered whether, in a decade or two, we might have huge central generators of electric power linking houses throughout London with the amazing new light source.

Holmes performed the same minute inspection of seat 62 and slipped another envelope into his pocket. "There are tiny holes in the front and back of the two seats, Mr Carte. I would suggest that you replace the upholstery and stuffing, taking care that your people do not inhale any dust, and then burn the materials."

He smiled at me. "For now, with Watson playing the dead baronets, we might just cover the seats with thick cloths."

A door opened at the side of the stalls and a group of people in mourning clothes entered and stood in front of the stage looking about them uneasily. I followed Holmes and Mr Carte down the stairs and I joined the mourners as the lights came up and Holmes strode to the front of the stage.

"Ladies and gentlemen of the Montague family," said Holmes. "I have asked you here to refresh your memory with regard to the evenings last week and in January when you attended a performance of *Ruddigore*. You will sit in the same seats that you occupied on that occasion. Doctor Watson will act as Sir Rutgar in seat 62 in the Gallery, and then as Sir Redvers in seat 47 in the stalls."

Pages ushered two separate groups of three people through the otherwise empty auditorium, one to the stalls on the right, the other into the Gallery high up on the left.

Holmes, Mr Carte and I followed the Sir Rutgar group up into the Gallery. The young lady who had admonished me the previous January was in the second seat from the aisle, three seats back. She gave me a cold look. Another lady and a gentleman that I presumed were also relatives of the deceased took their seats, leaving one seat vacant. Mr Carte covered it with a black cloth, a gesture that I saw was appreciated by the relatives of the deceased (and by me). I lowered myself gingerly into the poisoned chair.

"Why, incidentally was Sir Rutgar in the Gallery?" Holmes asked the baronet's niece.

"It was the opening night and he had left his booking rather late. There were no tickets left for the stalls. He was recovering from a bout of pneumonia (he had not been well all summer). He felt a little better, came up to Town and conceived the idea of a theatre visit on a whim as a treat for me and my cousins." The girl wept quietly into her handkerchief, and the young gentleman comforted her.

"He left his booking late? That is interesting," said Holmes. "Now, ladies and gentleman, I would like you to think back to that evening in January. Did anything untoward or unusual happen as you entered the theatre and took your seats, or later during the performance?"

The mourners looked blankly at each other.

"Did you notice the people in the row behind you? Were they male or female, single or a group?"

Again they had nothing to offer.

Holmes turned to Mr Carte. "Can we determine who booked the seats behind?"

He shook his head. "The Inspector asked me, and I had our records examined. Those seats, and indeed most of the Gallery were sold on the night. We have instituted numbered tickets, but on a first-come basis, with no identification required. The stalls are mostly pre-booked. We determined that Mr W H Smith, the First Lord of the Treasury and party, bought the six seats behind Sir Redvers." He coughed. "Inspector Gregson has been in touch with them, but they noticed nothing untoward that evening until Sir Redvers was taken ill."

Holmes nodded and turned once again to the bereaved family. "Close your eyes if you will, and try to recall —"

"There was a rude young man," said Sir Rutgar's niece. "A young man pushed along the row behind. He fell against Uncle's seat and Uncle jumped up and remonstrated with him. The man apologised and moved farther along."

"When was this exactly?"

"Just before the overture, as the lights dimmed."

Holmes eyes gleamed. "Which way was he passing?"

"From the aisle," the girl answered. "Behind us from our right to our left."

"What did you see of the man? He was young, you say; was he a boy, or a young man?"

"Early twenties, no more than twenty-five certainly."

"In evening dress, of course. Was there anything else about him? Was he carrying or holding anything?"

The girl looked at her companions and they shook their heads.

"Wait," said the young man next to me. "I recall that there were no free seats in the row behind. I thought it was deuced impolite of him to push along the row rather than use the aisle at the back of the Balcony."

"Excellent," said Holmes, rubbing his hands together.

His interrogation of the members of Sir Redvers family, seated in the stalls, with me acting as Sir Redvers, elicited a similar story. A young man had pushed along the row behind, banging into Sir Redvers' seat. Holmes pitted each family against the other and further details were recalled. The man was under twenty-five, pale but handsome, with a thin moustache and short black hair, centre-parted. He carried something, but no-one could recall what.

As Holmes and Gregson conferred by the orchestra pit, the lady on my left touched my arm. "Thank you, Doctor, for your efforts to catch my husband's murderer," she said softly.

I hurriedly extended my condolences to Lady Redvers. I asked if the young man and woman in the seats to my left were her children.

She shook her head. "Cousins. There is one child, a boy by Redvers' first wife, but we have never really seen eye-to-eye; I do not expect that Renulph will have mellowed in his time abroad. He has ignored my letters, defying his father's instructions. And now that Redvers is deceased, Renulph has sent instructions via our solicitors that I must vacate the estate in Cheshire. I was adequately provided for in Redvers' will and we have been there less than a year, but I love the Manor, Doctor. It is full of fond memories of my husband, although he was unwell most of the time."

"You married Sir Redvers after the death of his first wife, Renulph's mother?" I asked.

"That is correct, when Renulph, was sixteen. It is an awkward age. His mother had been deceased for nine years; I did not step into her shoes, Doctor. I thought it unwise to make the attempt, but I thought that we might be friends."

She sighed and dabbed her eyes with a scented handkerchief.

"Renulph was a handful and, as I have said, we did not get on. I attempted to construct a friendship between us, but it was not to be. Home life was, to some degree, disrupted by his coldness towards me."

"Was he sent away for —"

"He was not sent away. He had no aptitude for study; he did not want to attend university, or to join the family business here. South Africa seemed a fine opportunity; he has done well there."

Holmes interrupted us, thanked the family members for attending and said that they had been of material assistance. The parties left separately; there seemed to be no love lost between the two branches of the Montague family.

Holmes, Gregson and I repaired to The Coal Hole in the Strand.

"Who benefits?" asked Holmes as a waiter brought our drinks. "Two baronets have been eliminated. To whom does the estate devolve?"

"Renulph Montague," Gregson answered. "He is the son of Sir Redvers. But we cannot consider him a suspect; he has an unshakeable alibi. For the last seven years he has been resident in South Africa. He went to the Cape at the age of eighteen to help manage the family's mining and sugar refining interests there. He is now personal assistant to the managing director of the firm. I understand that he would have succeeded him, but for the unfortunate demise of his father."

I detailed what I had learned from Lady Redvers. "Every family has its black sheep, Holmes, but why was young Renulph sent away at such an early age? It seems odd."

Inspector Gregson sipped his beer and continued. "We interviewed the servants in Cheshire and in Eaton Square where the Montagues have their London home. The general opinion is that Renulph was a sensitive boy, a poet and over nice in his dress, but there was nothing bad in him."

"The murderer is a young man in his early twenties," I said. "Renulph was eighteen when he left this country for South Africa in 1880; if there is a connection, the murderer was but a boy when he knew Renulph."

"Unless they met in South Africa," Holmes answered. "Renulph is now twenty-five, the possible age of our murderer. I must send a cable to Cape Town."

"The new baronet is on his way home from by fast steamer," said Gregson. "He may be here any day."

Holmes frowned. "Why so? His father was murdered a few days ago. It is at least a twenty-five day passage from the Cape."

Gregson shrugged, and Holmes pursed his lips.

"How did the murderer know that the families were going to visit the Savoy on those particular days?" I asked as we returned home in a cab. "Sir Rutgar on the opening night, and then Sir Redvers. Sir Rutgar ordered his tickets at the last minute."

"You strike the nub of the question, Watson, as you so often do. There is a point of connection. Is it at the theatre, in the family houses, or at a club? Has a servant been suborned, or is the murderer an intimate of both families? I know there is a connection, my friend. We must find it."

"Montague," I said, looking out of the cab window as we passed a huge advertising hoarding. "Are they —"

"The family have extensive estates in the West Indies; the Montague warehouses and refinery are on the River at Wapping"

I stared at Holmes. "Sugar — one of the ingredients in our murder cocktail."

We arrived back home and found Billy at the bottom of the steps with a large wooden crate.

"Came from the University of London, sir, with eight shillings carriage to pay. Mrs Hudson used the float and had to borrow three bob from next door."

I helped Billy heave the crate up into our sitting room and watched as he unpacked dozens of books on toxicology.

"We must narrow our search," said Holmes as he leafed through a thick tome. "I borrowed these books from the University Medical Library (they owed me for that little matter of the bashful student last year)."

He slumped down into his chair in front of the fire. "What are the most usual reasons for murder?"

"Jealousy, money, revenge —"

"Precisely. Sir Rutgar Montague stayed most of the year at the manor in Cheshire, coming up to the City perhaps twice or three times a month. His brother, Redvers resided in Norwood, and visited Town even less frequently. They were not close; indeed they and their families did not speak."

"There must be some connection," I said. "It is strange. Even more strange is the sugar in the poison solution, and the fact that the Montague family fortune was originally based on sugar plantations."

Holmes nodded as Billy appeared at the door. "Here is coffee. You and I, Watson, shall get down to our studies. We want a colourless poison that acts within hours and with the symptoms of seizure, hallucinations and organ failure that the baronets suffered."

He grabbed an armful of books and settled into his chair.

I sipped my coffee and leafed through several books on Oriental poisons, but none fit the description of our agent. I lit my pipe and considered. I had heard of several vegetable alkaloids that acted swiftly and whose victims exhibited peculiar symptoms. I flicked through the index of a book on alkaloids and a pair of words sprang out at me: *castor beans*. I found the relevant page and read of the vegetable alkaloid *ricin*, a product of the crushing of the beans to make castor oil. It seemed a likely candidate, but the symptoms and speed of action were not — I stopped at a footnote. I scrabbled through the crate and found the book referenced, a book on poisons used as part of pagan rites. I read of an agent common in the West Indies where the Montague plantations were located.

"Holmes," I said in a shaking voice. "I may have it."

He looked up and raised an eyebrow.

"I suspected a natural alkaloid. I first thought that a poison obtained from castor beans might be our agent, but with *ricin* poisoning death usually occurs three to five days after exposure, and the symptoms do not fit. No, I think that the *rosary pea* may be our culprit. The plant is common in the tropics. Its seeds are bright red and they are astonishingly toxic, seventy or more times as lethal as *ricin*. The seeds are frequently used as beads in jewellery. A prick on the finger as the beads are being

70

threaded can and has had fatal consequences. The writer says that the beads are also used in the West Indies as a ghost repellent."

Holmes jumped out of his seat and pulled down the 'R' volume of his Index and flicked through it. "Nothing. The West Indies, you say?"

"Trinidad in particular. The ghosts in question are called *jumbies.*"

I passed him the book. "What now, Holmes?"

He frowned as he flicked through the pages. "We have the specimens from the Savoy, Watson. Now I know what enemy we have in our sights, I can refine my search with the help of the directions here. Well done, old chap."

I watched as he set to work with his chemicals and flasks.

I woke as the doorbell rang. It was dark, but Holmes still worked at his chemical bench by the light of an oil lamp. I stood and lit the gas as Billy knocked at the door and showed in a young man with a heavy black beard wearing a dark tweed suit with a thick mourning band around the sleeve of his jacket. He set his bowler hat and heavy stick on our sideboard.

"Good evening Sir Renulph," said Holmes, glancing up. "Pray take a seat for a moment while I complete this experiment. It is germane to your interests. Doctor Watson will fetch you a whisky, and I believe he still has a couple of excellent cigars from his man in the Strand."

I shook hands with Sir Renulph Montague, introduced myself properly, offered my condolences on his loss and ushered him to a chair by the fire.

Holmes put on a pair of my thick fishing gloves and picked up a dish from his work bench. "I shall not be a moment, gentleman. Watson, could you open the door?" He carried the dish reverently outside. "Billy! Fetch my mincemeat," he shouted down the stairs.

I was enquiring about Sir Renulph's voyage from the Cape when Holmes returned and sat in his accustomed chair.

"I went straight to Scotland Yard as soon as my ship docked, Mr Holmes," Sir Renulph said with a slight Cape Colony twang. "Inspector Gregson suggested that I contact you, and here I am."

Holmes leaned back in his chair. "Very well; you will forgive me if I get straight to the point? The murderer of your father and uncle is said to be a young man, in his early twenties perhaps. You have been away from England for seven years. Was there any person who might have felt wronged by you when you left these shores? You had just left school. Was there a younger boy there who had cause to dislike or even hate you or your family?"

The young man blinked at him. "The only younger boys one had contact with at school were fags, Elliott mostly, and the junior rugby eleven, who I helped coach. The rugby fellows were fine chaps and Elliott writes every now and then. He's at a small college in mid-Wales reading Theology, poor fellow."

I mixed our guest another whisky and soda. I could see that Holmes was in an interrogative mood.

"And after school?"

"I suppose I was something of a fop," the young man continued. "Very much a ladies man, in fact. I was to prepare for the university, but I spent my time in pubs, gambling dens and music halls —"

"And theatres? Did you visit the theatre before you left England? I refer specifically to Gilbert and Sullivan productions."

The young man shook his head. "Not my cup of tea. I prefer burlesques, variety acts and so on. The last act that I saw was Blondin the high wire man at the Crystal Palace."

He smiled. "I did visit the theatre, but not the inside. I waited at the stage door with the other 'johnnies' and with the obligatory chocolates and roses — the ladies of the chorus, you understand. I was young, well set up, with an ample allowance, and several of the ladies were kindly disposed towards me."

I smoothed my moustache as he continued.

"I was sent away by my father, on the advice of his brother, to break my connection with what they called unsuitable companions."

He shrugged. "I do not feel ill-used. I had no strong connections here in England and the experience of colonial life has made a man of me."

He sipped his drink. "As I have intimated, light opera is not to my taste, but I shall attend the final performance of *Ruddigore* at the Savoy on Monday."

I sprang up from my chair. "My dear Sir Renulph, is that wise? Your father and uncle were foully poisoned at performances of that opera. Is it not the greatest folly to subject yourself to danger for so trivial an entertainment? And frankly speaking, it is not one of the finer products of Sir Arthur and Mr Gilbert's collaboration. Mr Carte will revive the *Pirates of Penzance* after *Ruddigore*. I highly recommend that production over the current offering."

I helped myself to a bracing whisky and soda and resumed my seat as Holmes leaned forward in his chair.

"I believe that Sir Renulph will not attend *Ruddigore* entirely for pleasure, Watson. He has another purpose in mind. Is that not so?"

Sir Renulph nodded. "I am not the fawning milksop that I was when I left England, Mr Holmes. No man without steel in his backbone could thrive at the Cape. It would be a poor son and nephew who let the murder of his closest relatives go unpunished."

He opened his coat and revealed a large pistol in a shoulder holster.

"Revenge," Holmes mused. "We seem to have moved from *Ruddigore* to Elsinore."

He stood and helped himself to the last cigar from my packet. "Very well, if you are determined to play the bait, Watson and I will take post beside you. We must attend to our designs. First, the tiger must know that the goat is tethered."

"How did the murderer know that Sir Rutgar and Sir Redvers were to attend the play at the Savoy?" I asked again.

Holmes shook his head. "Any number of ways. Servants' gossip, perhaps. The mechanism by which he gathers intelligence is unknown, but we can make it easy for him. I will contact Langdale Pike, the Society columnist, and ask him to spread the news that an eligible young man has just returned from South Africa, and that he intends to spend time on his estates in Cheshire before returning to London in time for the last performance of *Ruddigore* at the Savoy. He will ensure that a paragraph and flattering picture appear in the illustrated papers."

Sir Renulph nodded. "Very well, but how do you know that the murderer wishes me harm, Mr Holmes? And do you not suspect that I arranged the deaths of my father and uncle to clear the way for my succession?"

Holmes smiled a jaguar smile.

"To your first question, I have to answer that I do not know for certain. It may be that the murderer or murderers had a grudge against your father and uncle and they are sated with Montague blood."

He leant back in his chair. "On your possible guilt, I had Inspector Gregson check the passenger lists of ships inbound from South Africa. You boarded a Clan Line steamer twenty-five days ago at the Cape and arrived here today. Newspaper records in Durban show you active in civic affairs in that town for at least the last three years. You cannot be considered a suspect in the poisoning of your father and uncle, unless you worked through intermediaries. I am having your cable traffic copied. You are no great letter writer, Sir Renulph; the *major domo* at your villa in Durban attested to local police that you sent and received very few letters, and that ones from your step mother were thrown into the fire unread. Your friend at theological college in Wales kept you up-to-date with cricket and rugby results by sending cuttings from the sporting newspapers."

Holmes smiled again. "You may see that I have not been entirely idle since I heard that you were on your way home."

The young man bowed.

"There is one more point," said Holmes. "You took ship from the Cape more than three weeks ago, well before your father's murder. Why were you hastening back to England?"

"I received a cable from my step-mother saying that my father was poorly (he was a martyr to gout) and I must come. I took the first available mail steamer."

I smiled, relieved that such a manly fellow, and an ex-rugby coach, was not a suspect in such a dastardly affair. I thought that I might invite him to watch the Club versus Oxford at Merton later in the month.

Our pageboy saw Sir Renulph out and into a cab. Billy reappeared in our doorway a few moments later and gave Holmes a thumbs-up. Holmes grinned, rubbed his hands together and turned to me.

"There are three elements present in the mixture injected into the baronets, distinguished by fineness of texture and colour variation. Two are simply powdered chalk and sugar — a few particles only. With those particles removed, I rendered a white powder. That is our poison. I mixed less than a half a grain of the substance with mincemeat and laid a trap for our rat, General Gordon, who was causing so much mayhem in the box room upstairs. The general took the bait and died."

He looked at his watch. "Billy will dispose of the body, and your gloves, in the hot water furnace."

"I say, Holmes. Those were my favourite fishing gloves."

Holmes and I arrived at the Savoy in a police carriage with Inspector Gregson opposite us. We alighted at the river front entrance. A man in a grey suit and wide-awake cap stepped from behind one of the trees outside. Gregson nodded to him and he disappeared again.

"I have plain clothes men at every entrance and exit of the House, gentlemen. Any young chaps, especially those not in company, will be tagged and followed."

Holmes led the way through into the auditorium and surveyed the stage.

"Do you think he will strike, Holmes?" I asked.

He considered. "If our man has any sense of the dramatic, he will not be able to resist the notion of a hat-trick of murdered Montagues at the Savoy."

"We have Sir Renulph in a front row seat," said Gregson. "Me on his left, and you and Doctor Watson on his right, with three of my staunchest constables in the row behind him. We have the entrances to the auditorium guarded and we have received a dispensation from Mr D'Oyly Carte to keep the electric globes burning through the overture and the start of Act 2. If chummy makes a move, we'll have him."

76

Holmes nodded as we took our seats. "Kindly remind your men that the assassin is armed and dangerous. He wields a syringe device containing one of the deadliest toxins known to man. He has murdered two men that we know of."

"Baronets," I reminded him.

"Commoners," he countered.

The overture started and nothing untoward occurred through most of Act 1. I thought that the play ran rather more smoothly than it had at the premier — as was only to be expected — but I noticed that Sir Renulph's head nodded and Inspector Gregson had to pinch himself to stay awake. The final chorus of the first act began with a crowded stage as a wedding was celebrated.

I heard a sudden cry and I turned to a disturbance at the left side of the auditorium. A tall man fell, and a slim man ran down the aisle and along the back of the orchestra pit in front of us. Holmes leapt up and collared the man, but Sir Renulph woke, misunderstood the situation, and tackled Holmes to the floor. The slim man was gone when I looked up, and Sir Renulph was on the carpet clutching his face.

"Powder," cried Holmes. "He sprayed powder onto Renulph's face."

I called loudly for water, and a stage hand staggered out of a side entrance with two full fire buckets. I turned Sir Renulph over, and dashed water over his face.

A cry came from the side of the auditorium as the lights came up and the audience stirred anxiously. Another man, a plain-clothes police constable had been attacked. His face was covered in white powder. More buckets arrived and I flung the contents onto him and called for more.

The house lights were turned up fully, and Mr Carte came to the front of the stage to reassure the audience and restore calm. He was seconded by Mr Barrington in his commanding, if faintly flat, baritone.

Holmes helped Sir Renulph through the crowd and out into the corridor. I aided Gregson to carry his man. "To the lavatory," I called. "Soak them, and yourselves."

"What is the prognosis?" Holmes asked as we watched stage hands pour water over the recumbent figures of Sir Renulph and the policeman.

"I do not know, Holmes. I have had no experience in this class of poisons. According to the literature, it does not need to be injected to be effective. The constable received the full brunt of the spray, and I fear for him. Sir Renulph received a lesser dose, possibly because there was little left in the dispenser."

I frowned. Something stirred in the back of my mind. I felt a recollection of the edge of my memory, but it was gone in a moment.

"He was a cool customer, our young friend," said Gregson. "And a lithe fellow. He realised that he was being followed, so he sprayed young Wicks, slithered past me and another of my lads, did the business with the baronet and scarpered. He must have known that we had the exits covered, but he got in and out of the auditorium somehow."

He smiled a grim smile. "But not out of the theatre. My men swear that no young man, alone, with another, or in a group, passed the outside doors. I have men scouring the auditorium and backstage. We are organising a sweep of the theatre, top to bottom; we'll get the beggar."

His tone hardened even further. "I won't have one of my young coppers injured and not get the blighter that did it. God help him when I get the derbies on him."

Holmes nodded. "He must have a plan of escape. Watch out for a bogus policeman or theatre workman."

A constable came up and spoke quietly to Gregson; he carried a top hat.

Gregson peered at the hat, shrugged and handed it to Holmes. "This was found in a ladies' retiring room on the other side of the entrance. Maybe chummy dropped it or threw it into the lavatory as a blind."

Holmes pounced on the hat and examined it through his magnifying glass. "It is an opera hat, of course," he said, compressing the hat flat and then allowing it to spring to its full height again. "And of very finest silk: one of Henry Heath's better quality models, slightly taller than the usual. The owner of this hat has a small head." He put the hat on his own head to ludicrous effect.

"The inside band is quite encrusted with the remains of hair unguents, and with odd flesh-toned creams. The man's valet should be shot." He pulled out his magnifying glass and glared at the hat. "There are faint letters on the hat brim, what do you make of them, Watson?"

I stared through his lens. "I think I can make out a 'C' and an 'M', and perhaps an 'H'. And then a squiggle of letters beginning with — is that another 'C'?"

Holmes nodded. "It is. I suppose, as we are in the world of make-believe, of topsy-turvy, that we should make the obvious connection. Since we have Montagues, Inspector, you might like to check the electoral rolls for a Capulet."

I looked at him in astonishment, and he shrugged. "But the key point about this hat is that, compressed or not, the attacker was not carrying it when he sprayed your man and the baronet."

"To the cloakroom, Mr Holmes?"

"My thoughts entirely, Inspector; bring the hat."

I watched as Holmes and Inspector Gregson interrogated the young cloakroom attendants.

"Ticket four-oh-nine," said Gregson at last. "A young, handsome man, in evening dress of course, left this opera hat and a large carpet bag. Not heavy, probably containing clothes. That's odd, of course; why bring such an article to the theatre? He picked up his bag and hat just as the kerfuffle started in the theatre and people streamed out."

Gregson tapped his nose in a manner that reminded me instantly of Inspector Lestrade. "If he's carrying a bag of clothes, then he might not be a native of London. He might be staying at a hotel. I will make my inquiries at the cab stands and omnibus depots." He took out his notebook. "What was that name you mentioned, sir? Could you spell it for me?"

I smiled to myself as Holmes spelled Capulet. "I do not think you will find him in a hotel," Holmes said, "although a search of private lodging houses might be fruitful after certain inquiries I must complete. Might I borrow the opera hat, meanwhile?"

"Is there an antidote?" Holmes asked as a police van carried Sir Renulph and the injured constable to St Thomas' Hospital.

I shook my head.

I followed Holmes out through a cordon of police and onto the Embankment. A strange smell, both pleasant and unpleasant pervaded the air.

"Mr Rimmeil's scent factory is close by," said Holmes. "As is Burgess's Noted Fish-Sauce Shop."

"You think that the culprit escaped the net, Holmes. How did he avoid the guards at the doors?"

"He did not avoid them. He walked past them with a smile and perhaps a polite nod."

Holmes picked up a sheaf of evening newspapers from the kiosk in the Strand and pored through them under a gas light while I visited my tobacconist, restocked with a half-pound of

Ship's, a half-pound of my new blend and a packet of cigars; I tried to make sense of what had occurred at the Savoy.

"Let's take a cab, Watson. That is certainly what our quarry has done."

I hailed a hansom from the stand. "Where to Holmes?"

"To the music hall," he replied. "To the Hall across the Water."

"The Canterbury," I instructed the driver.

We alighted at the Canterbury Music Hall on the south side of the Thames in the Westminster Bridge Road. We entered the hall through an elaborately decorated foyer and bought our tickets. Holmes grumbled loudly about the cost of the Balcony seats as we were led upstairs by a waiter who noted our damp clothes and took our order for the cheapest house red wine with an impertinent sniff.

"I say, Holmes," I said looking through the menu. "Prices here rival the Criterion."

"The Hall across the Water is clearly angling for a more select clientele than its location in south London provides. I hope that the entertainment merits the cost. I see from the programme that tonight's performance is a special one commemorating Jenny Lind. She died the other day."

"We have missed the first half," I said.

Holmes tipped his hat forward, leaned back in his seat and ignored the stage while I endured a long and elaborately-costumed ballet and several conjuring acts.

The chairman banged his gavel and prayed for silence for the next act in which our own, inimitable, *lion comique*, Champagne Charlie would sing a well-known ditty dedicated to our boys in Upper Burma.

Holmes sprang to life, leaned over the rail and glared at the stage.

"There has been a change in the programme, Holmes," I said, peering at the booklet in the faint light. It should be our own, inimitable, *lion comique*, Champagne Charlie singing 'Strolling in the P'.

Holmes frowned.

"Judging by the accompanying illustration it means strolling in the Park. The programme explains that strolling there is a fashionable activity for swells."

A flourish of trumpets and a long drum roll heralded a troupe of young ladies in ballet costumes carrying Union flags. They marched across the stage to a stirring tune, then lined up and kicked their legs up *à la can-can*.

"I say Holmes," I murmured, smoothing my moustache. "This is not quite the thing, you know."

He smiled and nodded across the auditorium to a box on the other side of the Gallery above the chairman's bench. I immediately recognised the rotund form of the Prince of Wales, in company with a group of sumptuously dressed gentlemen and several ladies.

"The Duke and Duchess of Teck attend his Royal Highness," said Holmes. "Thus driving up ticket prices and making the Canterbury very much the thing. When I last came here I paid ninepence for a gallery ticket and now it's half a crown."

He shook his head. "I see that His Royal Highness and His party are eating oysters south of the River. Although there is an 'R' in the month, some instinct of self-preservation suggests that we should not emulate him. I am surprised that no legislation exists prohibiting the heir from such foolhardiness."

I turned back to the show as a handsome young man in the uniform of a Guard's officer marched on stage carrying an enormous Union flag and took up the refrain of the song.

Britain's our Isle of the Sea!
Yes, Britain's the Isle of the Sea!
With Scotland, Ireland, Wales,
She never, never fails,
And shouts throughout the world for Libertee!"

With a final ta-ra-ra and another *can-can*, the officer marched the ballet dancers off-stage as a squad, swinging his swagger stick and singing.

Champagne Charlie is my name;
Good for any game at night, my boys,
Who'll come and join me in a spree?"

"Another change from the programme," said Holmes tapping the collapsed opera hat on his knees. "No self-respecting swell would stroll in the P without his topper."

We endured Ben and Bert comic jugglers, a troupe of Chinese acrobats and a tramp whistler. Holmes ignored them. The chairman banged his gavel again. "To bring a touch of class to our proceedings I would like you to welcome your own, your very own, Corinda Lebeau, singing a tuneful ditty that you will all recognise."

Holmes stretched and leaned over the balcony rail as a very pretty young girl tripped across the stage twirling her parasol in a highly-suggestive way. She pouted, sighed and sang.

"I'm a young girl, and have just come over,
Over from the country where they do things big,
And amongst the boys I've got a lover,
And since I've got a lover, why I don't care a fig."

The girl looked keenly up at the Gallery, and I saw the Prince of Wales smile down at her. He reached into his sleeve and took out a large white handkerchief as the orchestra played a familiar tune and Corinda sang again.

"The boy I love is up in the gallery,
The boy I love is looking now at me,
There he is, can't you see, waving his handkerchief,
As merry as a robin that sings on a tree."

I saw His Highness frown as the girl on stage sighed again, and sang next verse of the song to the Stalls without looking up.

Now, if I were a Duchess and had a lot of money,
I'd've given it to the boy that was going to marry me.
But I didn't have a penny, and you can't live on love and kisses,
And be just as happy as the birds on the tree.

Corinda looked again at the Gallery with what seemed to be more a mournful than a merry smile. The Prince beamed and fluttered his handkerchief, but the girl's gaze seemed to range past him and towards us. To my astonishment, she settled on Holmes and sang the final refrain of the song directly to him.

The boy I loved was up in the gallery,
The boy I loved was looking then at me,
There he was, you can't see, waving his handkerchief,
As merry as a robin that sings on a tree.

"I say, Holmes those aren't the right words —"
He stood and bowed to the singer on stage. The Prince of Wales glowered across the auditorium, the Duke and Duchess of Teck looked apprehensive and I saw the bald and hugely

moustached Duke of Cambridge peer around the Prince and blink at Holmes through his opera glasses.

Holmes stood. "Come on, old chap. Let us join the stage door johnnies."

I hurried after Holmes down the stairs as the chairman announced the next act, Doctor Orinoco and his dog, Coffee. We crossed the lobby, and, as I glanced at a poster for a ballet the following week, it came to me. I took my friend by the shoulder and stopped him.

"Holmes, I saw *A Midsummer Night's Dream* at the Crystal Palace when I was a lad. You know, with the Mendelsohn music."

"You are thinking of the fairies, Puck in particular."

"Yes! Puck sprinkled magic dust from a flower onto, well pretty much everybody — it was a *ballet comique* — and it came from a sort of wand with a flower attached."

Holmes nodded. "You have it, Watson. Puck sprayed chalk dust."

He marched on. "I do not expect a sudden flight, but I do not know our quarry well. We may have a flighty bird." He collared a page and asked directions. The boy led us backstage to a dingy corridor lined with doors, each of which was adorned with a faded gold star. He indicated one door, gave us an impertinent leer and held out his hand.

I placed a thruppenny bit on his palm, and he looked at it as if it was a bent farthing, but I remained resolute.

A soft *'Entre'* came from behind the door; I opened it and followed Holmes inside.

The beautiful young girl who had sung to Holmes sat at a dressing table, surrounded by vases of roses, dabbing at her face with a cloth. He looked at Holmes and I in her mirror and smiled a sweet smile.

"Miss Corinda," said Holmes. "I am —"

"I know who you are, Mr Holmes. You have quite a following among the artistes in the halls."

"Thank you. Watson, may I introduce Miss Corinda Lebeau?"

I bowed.

Holmes indicated a sofa. "May we?"

"Of course," she said with another brilliant smile. "We must have some Champagne. Perhaps your friend would order from the boy outside?"

I opened the door and found the same impudent boy leaning against the wall outside.

"Ginger beer, is it sir?"

I ordered Champagne and closed the door on the insolent wretch.

"Renulph Montague," said Holmes, as I joined him on the sofa.

Miss Lebeau sighed a sweet sigh. "I was at the Alhambra. Renulph was young, so was I (just seventeen summers). He showered me with gifts — the usual, chocs and roses, but also this." She held up a string of pearls.

"And this." She showed us a gold ring set with a brilliant. Her accent was hard to place, but I guessed American, or perhaps Canadian.

"We were very young." She turned from the mirror and sang.

"I'm a young girl, and have just come over,
Over from the country where they do things big"

"From America," said Holmes. "But originally from —"

"Trinidad. My father worked for Renulph's company over there.

"Sugar," I said.

"I was doing well; I could have had my pick." She saw my expression and shrugged. "Not for marriage, of course, but for high-class keeping: a house in Brixton and an account at Liberty's. I can still bait a hook; you saw Eddie out there. Ha, he was livid. I'd watch your step with Prince Eddie, Mr H, for he's got a temper on him."

She tapped Holmes on the knee and giggled. "Never mind. He'll come around. They always do. He has a carriage waiting for me at the stage door every night."

The door opened and the pageboy placed a wine cooler containing a bottle of Champagne with three flutes on a side table. He whistled *Champagne Charlie* as he handed me the bill. I gritted my teeth, paid the inflated price and ignored his sneer at my niggardly tip.

Holmes popped the Champagne cork with his usual dexterity. I handed a glass to Miss Lebeau and received a look that made me blink and smooth my moustache.

"Renulph proposed of course," Miss Lebeau continued with a sigh. "And for a moment or two I suppose I took him seriously. But Uncle Rutgar found out about us from the doxy he kept, and he told Sir Redvers that his son was engaged to a chorus girl (which I was then), and that was that. Renulph was whisked off to the Cape." She moved a vase of flowers and picked up a packet of cigars. "Roses, roses; I make it perfectly clear that I prefer violets, but they won't be told."

She offered Holmes and I cheroots, and, when we refused, lit her own cigar with practised ease.

"I was broken-hearted to the conventional degree and for the conventional period of time, but I got over it. My love died inside me when my cruel sweetheart boarded the ship for the Cape without a note, without a word."

"You determined on revenge," I suggested.

She giggled. "Oh, you think I killed Renulph, his uncle and his daddy for unrequited love!"

She sipped her wine, not the first of the day I thought, and shook her head. "No, no. It wasn't me that did Renulph and his relations. It was Charlie."

I blinked at her, and Holmes smiled.

"He did it. His grandmother was an Obi-women, a wise lady. She taught him all the tricks. He got some jequirity beads (rosary beads some call them), ground them down and made a powder and a solution. He nicked a wand from props and soon Rutgar was your late uncle."

She passed her glass to me to be refilled.

"Charlie's cold; very cold is Charlie. He's no feelings about him, but he has a strong sense of duty. He would never shirk his duty, not Charlie."

She patted some powder on her cheek. "I should explain that ours is a purely professional relationship."

Holmes held out the opera hat. "I think he dropped this."

"Thank you, Mr Holmes. We get charged by the Canterbury for lost props." She dropped the hat on her dressing table and took the glass I proffered. "Charlie did Redvers at the Savoy. It was easy to buy a cheap ticket, then wiggle down to the stalls and squeeze along the aisle behind him. A quick jab did for daddy. Charlie saw the notices in the papers about Renulph, and he sensed a trap. He thought he'd not be able to get as close as he wanted, and he might not get a jab in. So, he used powder instead. How is Renulph, Mr Holmes? Is he well? He was a bit of a softy, but I liked him, I really did."

"He is gravely ill in hospital," I answered, "but likely to survive."

She sighed. "Good for Renulph, I'd not have thought he had it in him."

"What about the parallels with *Ruddigore?*" I asked. "The baronets?"

Miss Lebeau frowned. "The opera on at the Savoy? Charlie never saw it. He just sneaked in the theatre, jabbed and tiptoed out." She picked up a dainty watch from her dressing table.

"Dearie me, I must get on." She patted her hair. "It's late supper at the Cafe Royal tonight, and Teck and Cambridge will be there."

I gave her a puzzled look. "The person who attacked all three baronets was a professional associate —"

Corinda convulsed with laughter. She whipped off her golden wig to reveal short, black hair, pressed a fake moustache under her nose, sprang the opera hat open and put it on her head.

"Champagne Charlie is my name,
Champagne Charlie is my name;
Good for any game at night, my boys,
Who'll come and join me in a spree?"

She laughed again as I gaped at her in astonishment, and then her face took on an anxious, cunning expression.

"He thirsted for revenge, did Charlie; it was his duty, of course. I suppose it's the rope for him?"

Holmes pursed his lips and said nothing.

She nodded and picked a hypodermic from her dressing table. "I still have the hypo intended for Renulph. I must take care with it gentlemen, for the slightest nick will kill. But it keeps the *jumbies* away."

She smiled a slight smile and plunged the hypodermic into her arm. I darted forward, but Holmes gripped my arm with an iron grip.

Corinda looked me directly in the eye. "I am a dead girl, Doctor, but they won't hang Charlie, will they?"

I shook my head as she took up the refrain again.

"And amongst the boys I've got a lover,
And since I've got a lover, why I don't care a fig
Eddie is his name and —."

She smiled. "You know, he sends a carriage for me every night, well, nearly every night." Her head fell forward and she lapsed into unconsciousness.

A messenger brought Inspector Gregson and a squad of policemen. Holmes and I stood in the corridor as the inspector examined the scene.

"How did she know when the baronets were going to the Savoy to see *Ruddigore?*" I asked.

"I did not ask, but I rather think Miss Roberts and both the older baronets were on intimate terms. She knew when they were coming up to Town."

"Scoundrels," I exclaimed.

"We might leave this to Gregson," Holmes said, leading me away.

"He says that Renulph is likely to survive, but the constable is feared for," I answered. "He has promised to take every precaution." I stopped in my tracks. "You deduced the Canterbury from the initials on the hat brim, and you checked the papers for a cross-dressing act."

"Corinda and Charlie."

"Sugar, Holmes! Where did the sugar come from?"

"The pantomime fairy dust; it adds sparkle." Holmes checked his watch. "We have missed the roast at the Criterion. How about the Cafe Royal?"

I looked at my toes. "I'm not sure that I am very hungry, Holmes."

He nodded and took my arm. We strolled out into the Westminster Bridge Road. The night was cold, and the street deserted, but for a providential hansom cab.

Holmes whistled, and the cab drew up. "Let us go home, then, old friend. We'll manage with pot-luck from Mrs Hudson, share our last bottle of Madeira in front of the fire and smoke a convivial pipe or two."

I climbed into the cab and Holmes jumped up after me. "That new blend from your man in the Strand is really rather good."

###

A Scandal in Tite Street

It was a dismal, cold and cloudy morning a few days before Christmas. Sherlock Holmes and I sat in front of the merry fire in the living room at our home in Baker Street; he read a volume of Petrarch while I flicked languidly through the latest *Lancet* and dozed intermittently. Neither of us had many friends to whom we owed season's greetings, and Holmes's practice as a detective, and mine as a doctor, were at that time, a few weeks after the start of our acquaintance, still in the bud rather than fully in bloom. Holmes' regular trickle of visitors from all classes and walks of life had almost dried up before the holiday, and I, not fully recovered from the effects of my wound and its debilitating aftermath, was of a sedentary disposition and, if truth be told, rather tetchy on cold days when my wound bothered me. I could go as far as to say that both Holmes and I were at a loose end (criminals having taken time off for the festivities) and that a long ring at the doorbell of 221B was greeted with expectant smiles.

"A man," said Holmes, women know the value of bell wire. A vehement ring; he is mine, rather than yours, I think."

We heard a heavy tread on the stairs and our sitting-room door opened wide to reveal a strange, even alarming figure. He was a tall man in a wide-brimmed floppy hat, a long black coat trimmed with astrakhan and gleaming leather gloves. His coat was open, and beneath it he wore a crushed velvet tunic with satin knee breeches, beribboned silk hose and pump shoes. A white lily adorned his buttonhole. His pale face, under an unruly mop of long hair, was oval, and his expression was cold.

The man stepped into the room and, assuming a theatrical pose, regarded our humble sitting room with evident distaste. He turned to me. "Mr Sherlock Holmes?"

"That's me," Holmes replied in his casual manner, waving from his chair.

The man pulled off one of his gloves and flung it to the floor at Holmes' feet. "My friend will contact you in due course," he said in a tight tone.

Holmes peered at the glove over the top of his book and looked up again. "Would you care for tea?"

The man glared at him, turned, marched past our page boy and stomped down the stairs.

Holmes picked up the glove and tossed it to Billy. "Give that back to the gentleman, and inform him that he forgot to leave a calling card."

Billy scampered down the stairs.

"Extraordinary behaviour," I exclaimed. I went to the window and looked down on Baker Street. The man was whistling for a cab. I saw Billy run up to him, pluck at his sleeve and hand him back his glove. He seemed rather taken aback, but he pocketed the glove, took something from his waistcoat pocket and handed it to the boy. The man looked up at our window as Billy ran back inside; he saw me and (I can only think of one word to describe his action) flounced away.

"Extraordinary behaviour," I repeated. "The fellow must be mad."

"Highly agitated, certainly," said Holmes. "Otherwise he would have left his card with the page and arranged for his cab to wait. He will have trouble getting a hansom; I can smell fog in the air."

There was a thunder on the stairs, and Billy appeared in the doorway wearing a wide grin and triumphantly holding up a calling card. I sighed. "I have told you twice, young man, that you must ascend the stairs in a seemly manner and that letters and cards are presented on the silver tray that is laid conveniently on the hall table by the front door."

Billy's grin died and he looked down at his shoes. "Which, the tray is with Missus getting polished. I'll fetch it."

He grinned again, and disappeared, thundering down the stairs.

"Missus?" asked Holmes.

"Mrs Hudson. Really, Holmes, I do not think the boy will do. He is graceless, too young, too —"

Holmes waved away my concerns, stood and filled his pipe from my pack of *Ship's* on the mantel. "What of our visitor?"

"We'll know when Billy brings the card."

"What can we tell from the gentleman's appearance and manner?" Holmes asked, lighting his pipe from the fire with a spill.

I sighed. In the few weeks that I had known Sherlock Holmes I had learned that, like my bulldog pup, Gordon, he would never let go once he'd sunk his teeth into something. Holmes had to squeeze and drain each fact and circumstance of every ounce of data before he indulged in the peculiar style of wild speculation that he called deductive reasoning.

"He was a flamboyant figure," I answered Holmes. "He wore an astrakhan-trimmed coat with dancing pumps! Ha! An actor perhaps, or a foreigner, or a foreign actor! He sneered at our poor sitting room like a European aristocrat; yes, that's it: he is a Bohemian aristocrat. Judging from his hair, I'd say an archduke at the very least."

Holmes smiled. "Would you say that his dress and demeanour were aesthetical at all?"

"Like the fellows in that Sullivan and Gilbert frivolity, *Patience*, earlier in the year? Like Swinburne, that writer fellow one reads about?"

"Possibly."

"He did not seem impressed by our furnishings." I looked around the sitting room that Holmes and I had recently come to share. Stacks of books and piles of papers covered both Holmes' desk and my own; uncleared breakfast dishes adorned our dining table, a clasp knife secured Holmes' correspondence to the mantel and a reeking lab bench stood in one corner of the room cluttered with the vials and instruments with which Holmes performed his chemical experiments. While not quite shabby, our rooms already, after only a couple or so months of habitation, looked rather well-worn.

"Lived in," said Holmes.

I sniffed and opened a fresh page in one of the notebooks in which I had taken to recording the singular occurrences that Holmes seemed to engender even in our quiet corner of Baker Street. I had hoped to find a quiet nook in which to recover from my wound and repair my nerves, shattered by my experiences in the Afghan War. I had found that living with Mr Holmes was by no stretch of the imagination a rest cure.

Billy crept up the stairs and slipped into the room holding out our half-polished salver with a single card on it. I snatched it up. "It says 'Mr Oscar Wilde, One, Tite Street, Chelsea'. I've never heard of the fellow."

Holmes considered. "I read of him in the illustrated newspapers. He is known for walking in the West End in a similar attire to the one in which he presented himself to us today, but with a large sunflower as a *boutonnière*."

"What can you have done to offend the fellow, Holmes? I know you move in a remarkably diverse array of social circles, but I had not thought aestheticism was in your line at all."

Holmes shrugged. "Wilde is Irish. The Celts call each other out for the most trivial of reasons. Perhaps I bumped into him in the Strand, or stepped ahead of him in the queue at the newsagent's."

I took my pipe from the rack. "Take care: he may be a Parnellite: a supporter of Home Rule for Ireland; a Fenian dynamitard of the worst possible hue."

"How do you know that I am not?" Holmes asked. He passed me my packet of tobacco from the mantel.

I laughed and then frowned at him. "I mean, you're not. Are you?"

"I have no opinion on the matter, other than that our stewardship of that benighted country has been incompetent and at times, beastly. If I were Irish, I believe I would be a passionate revolutionary. As it is, I shall leave it to the professionals."

He stood. "Talking of whom, there is one authority whose expertise I must employ. I believe he may have the key to our riddle, or at least know where it might be found. You have full-dress rig, I imagine. Dust it off, and we shall accept the Duchess of Coulteney's invitation to her Christmas rout this evening." He hunted along the mantel and found a large cream-coloured card pinned to the mantelpiece by his clasp knife. He removed the card and flattened it on the table. "It is a little smudged, and slightly ripped but it will do."

"Rout, Holmes?"

"Reception. Lady Audrey's rout cake is much appreciated by connoisseurs; wear your pumps: there may be dancing."

I frowned.

"Oh, my dear fellow," said Holmes, grasping my arm. "I apologise. I saw you moving about much more freely than before and I assumed that your wounds were troubling you less. Sit you down and I shall get you a blanket."

I shrugged off Holmes' helping hand. "I am perfectly fine, within limits. I shall certainly accompany you to Lady Audrey's, but I cannot promise dancing."

Holmes smiled. "Never say die, old man, you may yet

—trip it as ye go,
On the light fantastick toe."

"How do you know the Duchess of Coulteney, Holmes?" I asked as our hansom turned into Park Lane and joined the queue of carriages dropping guests at her door.

"I do not; I performed a small service for her butler, Hampson, and Her Grace was grateful. She sends me invitations to all the grand parties and balls. This is the first time I have taken one up."

I shook my head in amazement. "You constantly surprise me, Holmes."

"And you me, Doctor: you look very fine in your evening dress. Your tiepin is singular; it was your great, great grandfather's of course. Ah, here we are."

Holmes helped me down from the cab and waited while I paid the cabby. The usual crowd of low gawkers had assembled at the bottom of the steps to the open front door of the Coulteney mansion. They peered into the brightly lamp-lit lobby and offered admiring or ribald comments as gentlemen and ladies alighted from their carriages and made their way inside.

As I followed Holmes up the marble steps I stumbled slightly and grabbed the railing.

"Gawd luv us," came a high-pitched cry from a person in the crowd. "Here's a nob drunk as a lord before he even gets inside."

I turned and frowned as the crowd erupted with laughter. A young boy in a flat hat waved at me and grinned.

"Come along, Doctor," said Holmes, offering his arm.

"I say, Holmes. I know that boy. Is he not —"

"Wiggins, the leader of the Baker Street Irregulars. He is here to look out."

I gave my coat, hat and gloves to a servant, who seemed perplexed for some reason, and passed through the Great Hall with its grand staircase and huge Chinese vases full of hothouse flowers. We were announced at the door of a superbly-decorated room in which the light from crystal chandeliers was brilliantly reflected in the mirrored walls. A highly-ornamented Christmas tree standing in a niche by the fireplace added the glow of hundreds of candles. The room was crowded, and I followed closely behind Holmes as he slipped through the crush towards the far corner. He seemed to know several of the finely-dressed gentlemen and even more of the richly-bejewelled ladies.

We passed by a group of political gentlemen and I saw the tall figure of our prime minister, Mr Gladstone, pause in his conversation and bow a greeting to Holmes, which he returned. The Prime Minister was in conversation with two young men in midshipmen's uniforms; I recognized the princes Albert Victor and George, teenage sons of the Prince of Wales. I had read in the journals that they were with a cruiser squadron on a three-year goodwill tour of the world. They were evidently home on Christmas leave.

I followed Holmes to the far corner of the room in which Langdale Pike, Holmes college friend, lounged against a marble pillar and regarded the crowd over the rim of a tea cup. He shook my hand and nodded to Holmes.

"Holmes, my dear chum, how odd to see you in such august surroundings. You look quite the gentleman, my dear, dear fellow, apart from the chemical stains and plasters on your fingers and your peculiar cravat. It is an abomination; take it off at once and I will borrow a replacement from the bootboy. You remind me of a disgraced footman at the gas fitter's ball."

I twitched my own bow tie into better alignment.

"You found me in the crowd?" Pike said.

"Elementary," said Holmes. "I know that Christmas displays are anathema to your aesthetic sensibilities. I merely triangulated the room. This is the only nook from which that gigantic Christmas tree is invisible."

Pike nodded. "What a mound of gee-gaws and baubles it is, gentlemen; it is a Hessian *hausfrau's* vision of heaven. Did you note the statuette of St Anne on top of the tree? She represents Lady Audrey (the Coulteneys were a recusant Catholic family during the Elizabethan repressions). I am surprised that she has contented herself with a saint and not gone *jusqu'au bout* with an angel."

He smiled and nodded to a passing acquaintance. "You must make your number with our hostess, then we can find a quiet spot to have a nice chat." He frowned at me. "Doctor, where is your top hat? Where are your gloves?"

"I handed them to the servant in the hall with my coat." I held up a coloured ticket. "He gave me this." I looked around and saw to my horror that every gentleman in sight wore gloves and had his hat either in his hand or on a table or footstool beside him.

Mr Pike snapped his fingers at a liveried footman. He gave the servant my ticket, and instructions to retrieve my hat and gloves and meet us by the duke.

Mr Pike saw my consternation and he smiled, put a consoling hand on my arm and pulled back a lock of his hair to disclose a tiny gold ring that pierced his left ear. "I too defy convention to a very limited degree."

Holmes and I followed Mr Pike as he threaded his way through the crowd, bowing to acquaintances. Both he and Holmes seemed to glide effortlessly between groups of ladies and gentlemen, while I, somewhat encumbered by my stick, took care not to tread on the hems of the ladies' elaborate dresses. We reached another quiet niche adorned with a statue of Henry, Duke of Coulteney.

The servant returned with my hat, gloves and ticket. He looked me up and down as he handed them to me and smirked. I reddened, suddenly feeling quite out of my depth in the glittering throng around me.

"Come on, old man," said Holmes, taking my arm. "Let's meet our hostess."

We joined a short receiving line and we were introduced to Lady Audrey, Duchess of Coulteney and a bevy of young ladies that I presumed were her relations. The Duchess smiled weakly at me as she took my hand, and, as I returned her smile, it seemed to me that neither of us was having a terribly good time.

Pike, who was clearly perfectly at home in the Coulteney mansion, gave orders to a footman and led us across the entrance lobby and into a suite of rooms on the opposite side of the reception hall. We passed through a library and into a reasonable-sized room, bigger than our own poor sitting room, furnished with buttoned leather chairs and sofas. A great wooden desk dominated the space between the windows.

"His Grace's study." Mr Pike offered cigars from a silver case. "When the Duke was alive, no smoking was allowed in his presence." He lit his cigar with a match. "Lady Coulteney allows me to use the room for my cigars and literary exertions."

I knew that Holmes' friend wrote on Society topics for a number of newspapers and magazines.

"Whisky? Champagne is on its way."

Holmes and I settled for whiskies and soda. "Should you not be out there mingling with the nobility and picking up points of interest for your columns?" Holmes asked.

"No, no — ah here is the Champagne." A footman placed a wine cooler and glasses on a side table, together with a large cake. Mr Pike poured himself a glass of Champagne and passed slices of cake to Holmes and I. It was delicious.

"No," said Pike. "I will not mingle tonight. The Prince of Wales is here, either in the billiard room, or upstairs with Miss Bernhardt. The party is therefore a *succès automatique* and my column will say so; it is only when the Prince evades an invitation, or, worse, does not turn up, that I need to feel the pulse of the evening."

He smiled at Holmes. "We can speak privately in here. I deduce from your presence that you require my services in some little matter."

Holmes gave Mr Pike a succinct account of Mr Wilde's outlandish appearance and astonishing challenge.

Mr Pike considered. "Mr Wilde is a poet of the fleshly school. He has just published a slim volume of verse that was well reviewed. Other than that, he is known only for his outlandish dress. I have heard tell that he was the inspiration for Bunthorne in the Gilbert and Sullivan comic opera, *Patience*, but Mr Gilbert denies it. What more? Oh, yes, he is intimately associated with Lillie, of course."

Holmes and I looked at each other and turned back to Mr Pike.

"Oh, wait, wait!" I exclaimed. "Lillie Langtry, Holmes, the Society beauty; I heard that she has taken up acting."

"Mr Wilde urges her to become an actress," said Mr Pike with a chuckle. "She makes an effort, poor thing; the Prince sponsors her (they are no longer close, but he, not having to pay for his ladies' favours, is grateful in other ways) and so her performances are well-received."

"She was accepted into Society quite quickly, despite coming from the Channel Islands," I suggested.

Mr Pike sipped his Champagne and smiled. "You may think, Doctor, that there are fixed caste barriers; in fact, acceptance into Society does not wholly depend on birth and breeding, on personal riches or on personal charm; there is certainly no fastidiousness about manners, morals or intellectual gifts. But somewhere about you, or your dynasty, must be an indefinable something: the possession of some form of power perhaps. With a man, breeding, money and a certain stiffness of attitude might suffice. A striking woman has power over men; Society sees this power as not being much different from the authority of a politician who exercises his rule in Parliament, or a duke who presides over his estates. The Prince of Wales leads us, by rank, by wealth, and by his obsession with having fun: he is really quite broad-minded, even with regard to Jews and Catholics, and Society mirrors his bonhomie. I can assure you that our Continental equivalents, listed in the *Almanach de Gotha*, are considerably more rigorous in their exclusions."

He smiled again. "Why, I believe that I could take a common girl and after six-weeks coaching, I could enter her into Society with nobody the wiser."

Holmes laughed. "A flower girl from Covent Garden?"

Mr Pike sipped his Champagne and considered. "Yes, even such a creature; I would have her pass as a duchess; a European duchess, naturally."

"Of course."

"Come." He led us out of the study and along a sumptuously-decorated corridor and through an archway into a small reception room. A group of ladies and gentlemen clustered around a gilt-framed painting that stood on an easel under bright gas lights. It depicted a lady wearing a long black dress and holding a lily in her hand. We joined the ladies and gentlemen admiring the portrait.

The lady was pretty, I thought, but not conventionally beautiful. I peered forward and read the title on the frame. 'A Jersey Lily, by John Everett Millais'. I sniffed and turned to Holmes. "The young lady is not holding a Jersey Lily, Holmes. It is a so-called Guernsey Lily, *Nerine sarniensis*, not a lily at all, by right."

I realised that I had spoken too loudly and that a tall man glowered at me over the heads of the ladies. I started when I recognized Mr Oscar Wilde, dressed conventionally apart from his long, flowing locks and over-large lily *boutonnière*.

He turned from me with a sneer, adopted a theatrical pose and began to declaim a poem.

"The New Helen," Mr Pike muttered in my ear. "It is from his slim volume published earlier in the year."

> *"Yet care I not what ruin time may bring*
> *If in thy temple thou wilt let me kneel."*

I turned to Holmes with a remark, but a young man stepped in front of me and almost literally buttonholed me. "I am Frank Miles; I second Mr Wilde in his affair of honour with Mr Holmes. Might I ask you to kindly vacate the room? According to the rules of duelling, principals do not engage in social intercourse before the dread event."

I looked down on the man in astonishment. I stood erect, stiffened and made to slap the insolent fellow away, but Holmes quickly took my arm and steered me out of the room.

"What a fierce chap you are, Doctor," he said, chuckling, as we retraced our steps to the study. "I had no idea what a hot-tempered fellow lodger I had at 221B. I shall have to watch my step, I see."

I reddened again. "Infernal cheek, Holmes; ordering us from the room. I should have taken my cane to the wretch."

He smiled again, and I subsided as Mr Pike joined us.

"The painting is Lillie, of course," he said. "Wilde's poem is dedicated to her — to Lillie as Helen. When his *Poems* appeared, Wilde sent her a copy with the inscription: 'To Helen, formerly of Troy, now London' or some such rot. We understand that Mr Wilde composed the poem kneeling on the marble steps outside Madame Langtry's residence. Who could resist such devotion? He presents her with a lily each day, advises her on her clothes and coiffure, and is teaching her Latin."

"He is in love, or at the very least, infatuated with the lady," I suggested.

"Yes," said Pike with a decided sniff. "One might think so, or one might not."

Holmes spoke some lines of the poem from memory.

"But in this poisonous garden must I stay,
Crowning my brows with the thorn-crown of pain,
Till all my loveless life shall pass away."

Holmes considered. "Hmmm, 'thorn-crown', this Mr Wilde has high notions of himself."

"Indeed," said Mr Pike. "And perhaps he protests a little too much. When Lillie found herself in a certain condition last year, Mr Wilde was not suspected as the father, nor was her other patron, the portraitist Frank Miles, the person with whom Wilde lodges. I believe that Mr Wilde's amorous affections, when he is not being aesthetical, are bestowed in another direction entirely."

"Well." I said. "That is evidence in his favour; he is not a cad."

Holmes and Mr Pike looked blankly at me.

"He did not stoop to forcing his favours on his Latin pupil."

"Of course." Holmes chuckled and turned back to Mr Pike. "Who — ah?"

"Did the deed? Serious money is on Prince Louis of Battenberg," said Pike. "Lillie told His Grace that he was the father, the prince told his parents (he is twenty-seven years old and a Royal Naval officer) and they had him assigned to the appropriately named HMS *Inconstant* about to sail to South America. Miss Langtry received certain emoluments and retired with her husband to Paris for the birth: happily, a girl."

"Miss Langtry is married!" I exclaimed.

"To a degree."

"Come, Watson," said Holmes. "I see you are looking pale. Let us go home and see what Mrs Hudson can offer for late supper."

Mr Pike saw us to the door. As we collected our coats, he took me aside. "You know, I could introduce Holmes into Society, if he would only behave himself and not gad about with undesirables." He looked me up and down. "And yourself, Doctor, where is your practice? Harley Street?"

"Baker Street."

He shook his head and we bowed goodnight.

The following day, as Holmes and I smoked our after-breakfast pipes and leafed through the papers, there was a ring on our doorbell and a moment later the boy announced that a gentleman was in the waiting room downstairs and that he desired me to meet him there.

I gave Holmes a puzzled look. "Mr Wilde's second," he said. "He will not come up. He cannot talk to you in front of me."

"Ah, the annoying Mr Miles. I suppose I must meet him. I believe that the challenged party decide the weapons; do you have any preferences, Holmes?"

He shrugged and returned to his newspaper.

I stood. "Are you sure that there is nothing between you and this Mr Wilde? Nothing concerning a female person for example?"

"Concerning the honour of a lady?"

"Yes."

"I have never met Madame Langtry, I did not know of her until our conversation with Pike. I have met Mr Wilde twice, in the circumstances you know."

"It is an odd situation, Holmes."

"I am entirely in your hands, my dear fellow."

I found Mr Miles in our waiting room admiring a Chinese vase on the mantel. He wore conventional clothes, but his frock coat was adorned with an enormous orchid. He turned to me. "Oscar adores blue-and-white."

We made our formal introductions and I ordered tea.

"Well, Doctor," he began. "Mr Wilde lodges at my residence in Chelsea, and so here I am. I am afraid that I make a poor second as I know very little about duelling. I was a delicate child and my up-bringing was entirely sheltered and without any tincture of violence."

I frowned. "I can assure you, Mr Miles, that no-one knows less than I about the practice of duelling, even though I was a surgeon with the Army in Afghanistan. When one is being sniped at by *jezailchis*, one has more tolerance for the foibles of one's fellow officers who are also targets."

Mr Miles sniffed. "I know nothing of sniping; I had a very quiet childhood on the family estates; we did not shoot."

"It is not a question of —" I caught myself; my choler was rising fast, and I had my duty to Holmes.

Mrs Hudson came in with tea, which gave me a chance to regain my equanimity.

"Might I have some idea of the affront that Mr Holmes is alleged to have offered Mr Wilde?" I asked, as the door closed behind her.

Mr Miles stirred his tea and considered. "I regret to say that, on the matter of the challenge, I cannot speak. That is between the principals. However, I can say that an apology, couched in appropriate terms, would be perfectly acceptable to my man. Oscar is not a man of blood."

"Even if my man were willing (which I doubt), it would be difficult for Mr Holmes to apologise for something that he does not admit he did, to someone he does not know that he affronted — you catch my meaning?"

Mr Miles sipped his tea. "I can say that Mr Wilde is concerned that a certain person's honour has been, or might be impugned."

I leaned forward and lowered my voice. "Am I treading on dangerous ground here if I mention a — Madame L?"

"Oh, no, Doctor, you are on perfectly safe ground with me. According to my guidebook, seconds are not allowed to quarrel while on their principal's business; you may be frank."

I looked blankly at Mr Miles. "There is a guidebook?"

"*The Heavy Dragoon's Guide to Duelling*, the *code duello*, translated from the Prussian. I picked it up at a little place in the Charing Cross Road."

"I see. Can you tell me anything about Mr Wilde? As the challenged party, we have choice of weapons. We would like be as fair as possible to the challenger. Is he a sporting gentleman?"

"Does he shoot, you mean? No, I don't believe he does. Nor ride to hounds, fence or engage in manly sports at all. But, wait; at college he boxed, once at least. There was an incident with some rugby types who did not like his manners; he held his own with his fists."

"My man boxes."

"Well then."

"I should have to insist on gloves," I said. "The Marquess of Queensberry endorses their use."

Mr Miles grimaced. "I cannot stand the sight of blood. Agreed."

"And the venue?"

"That is usually the prerogative of the challenger, Doctor. Mr Wilde is in the Italian coffee shop over the way; might I, with your permission, consult with him on your pugilistic suggestion and the location of the fight?"

"And I with Mr Holmes." We stood and bowed to each other. There was an exasperating piece of almost Continental nonsense as Mr Miles and I each attempted to usher the other out of the door before him. We might have gone on bowing, scraping and gritting our teeth till the crack of Doom, had not quick-witted Billy spotted our dilemma, opened the street door and bowed to Mr Miles. Faced with two usherings, Mr Miles was trumped, and he allowed himself to be escorted outside. I hurried upstairs and acquainted Holmes with the fruits of our discussions.

Holmes languidly agreed to box Mr Wilde, and he suggested several venues that he thought suitable. I went downstairs and found Mr Miles had returned and was warming his coat-tails before our fire.

"My man agrees," I said. "He suggests the yard of *The Duke of Sussex* pub in Lambeth."

Mr Miles threw up his hands in horror. "South of the River!"

I referred to a note on my shirt cuff. "Or *The Ten Bells* in Whitechapel."

Mr Miles pulled a large white handkerchief from his pocket and mopped his brow. "I am afraid that Oscar would never agree to so *outré* a location. I have an idea. Let my side provide the venue, and yours the referee. The reception room in my house in Chelsea has a sprung floor and Doctor Heppel, the oculist, lives a few doors down, in case of need."

I nodded. "Agreed. We may bring supporters?"

"A reasonable number; we do not want a *fracas*." Mr Miles considered for a moment. "There is the question of dinner; I feel that for the participants to dine together before the duel, even at opposite ends of a long table, might be tiresome in view of the constraints on the principals. And there is always the chance of something untoward occurring. But the notion of dining afterwards is also somewhat fraught; there may be vestiges of ill-feeling and possibly unpleasant wounds that might put diners off their food and mar the occasion."

"What does your handbook advise?"

"Beer and sausages available during breaks between rounds; we may anglicise that to hot sherry punch and canapés, with your approval. My man will drink Champagne."

"Mine may smoke a cigar between rounds."

"Agreed."

"Well then —"

We stood. "Time and date?" Mr Miles asked. "I should mention that my man is booked on a steamer to America on Saturday. He has arranged with Mr D'Oyly Carte to give a series of lectures in cities throughout the United States on the subject of Aestheticism. Mr D'Oyly Carte wants to educate Americans on the subject of beauty in order that they may understand the

Gilbert and Sullivan operetta, *Patience* now opening in New York."

"I wish Mr Wilde the very best of success," I said doubtfully.

Mr Miles sighed. "It is a labour of Hercules, I must admit."

"Would tomorrow at ten in the morning suit?" I suggested. "That would give Mr Wilde a day or two to recover before his voyage?"

"Done, sir. And may I say that it has been a pleasure doing business with you?" Mr Miles reached for his hat and gloves, but stopped.

"Wait," he exclaimed. "We have not yet come to terms. According to my guidebook we must agree on the mechanism of defeat and victory. If your man wins, what? If mine, what then?"

I considered. "I can only repeat that Mr Holmes would find it difficult to apologise or make reparation for something that he does not admit he has done and when he does not know who, if anyone, has been wronged."

"A nice dilemma, Doctor. The handbook says that if an accommodation as to the winner cannot be effected, opposing seconds must, in honour, set to with rapiers."

We regarded each other with pursed lips. "I would say, sir," I suggested, "that for both our sakes we might inquire further into the facts behind this challenge. We require an injured party."

"Everything is settled, Holmes," I said as I slumped into my seat before a merry fire in our sitting room. We meet at Mr Miles' home in Chelsea tomorrow morning. I cannot say how happy I am that this affair will not be settled by bloodshed."

"You think that Mr Wilde and I will not 'tap the claret' as the Fancy put it?"

"I sincerely hope not."

"What did you think of Mr Miles?"

"A gentleman, but I was not charmed by his mincing ways. Too much the ladies' man, I fear. These fellows cultivate a philosophical, poetical air and airy damsels flock to them. It is vexing to those of us with more manly inclinations."

After luncheon, Holmes and I settled ourselves in front of the fire and considered the merits of my suggestion of an afternoon stroll through the Park. Holmes' fog had not appeared, and, although the day was overcast and cold, we decided that with Ulsters and scarves we would be well-enough armoured against the weather to venture out. Another long ring at the doorbell disturbed our plans. A moment later Billy stood in the doorway frowning at a calling card on the salver. "Prince Alexander of Butterberg, Battenberg, Prince of B—" A tall, handsome young man in a spade beard appeared behind the boy and whispered in his ear. "Prince of Bulgraria," said Billy with a bright grin and a sweeping bow.

The young man of perhaps twenty-five patted the boy on the head, strode into the room, placed a large carpet bag on our table, and stood arms akimbo and eyes gleaming over his luxurious moustache and beard. "I am Alexander," he said in a strong voice.

I stood. "Doctor Watson at your service, Your Highness." He held out his hand and we shook; he turned to Holmes.

"And you are Mr Sherlock Holmes, are you not sir?"

"I am." Holmes waved the prince to a chair. "Would Your Highness care for tea?"

"No, no," he exclaimed. "Of tea, an ample sufficiency I have had with my friends at the Palace."

"A whisky, perhaps?" I offered. "But we have no soda at present as our gasogene exploded again."

"A whisky with water would be kindly received, Doctor." He stood and marched across to the side table with me. "It is

111

often a question of joints, or sometimes of levers," he said as he examined the remains of our soda bottle. "We have, at the Royal Palace in Sofia, bottles made by a local firm that are tested to eight hundred pounds of pressure! Imagine! And the manufacturer is so confident of his glass that he has dispensed with the metal safety cage. I shall send you a dozen on my return to my princedom."

He took his whisky, returned to the sofa, leaned forward and addressed Holmes.

"Eddy speaks very highly of you, sir; he mentioned matters pertaining to certain crowned heads in Europe that you were active in, but hush, no more of that. When I learned of a delicate case regarding a sprightly correspondence that might embarrass a friend — I instantly thought of you."

"Eddy? Do you mean the Prince of Wales?" I asked.

The prince's eyes narrowed. "I do not so mean, Doctor. I would never in such a direct way speak of the Prince of Wales. No, no, I mean his teenage son, Albert Victor, whom we in royal circles call Eddy."

He took a sip of whisky. "He and his brother, George, are fine boys and my brother, Prince Louis and I consider ourselves their honorary uncles. There is not in age so much difference. Eddy is almost seventeen and I am twenty-four. Eddy is a follower of the crime papers, like his grandmother, the Queen. He talks of you often, Mr Holmes. He would rather be a detective than a naval officer, but naturally that cannot be."

Holmes bowed.

"Now, I come to you in regard to a matter of some, how can I say —

"Delicacy," I offered.

"Sensitivity. Certain documents are held at a residence in London, in Tite Street in Chelsea — what?"

Holmes smiled. "At One, Tite Street? The residence of Mr Frank Miles and Mr Oscar Wilde?"

The prince blinked at Holmes. "You know of this already?"

"Mr Wilde has challenged Mr Holmes to a duel," I answered.

"Ha!" The prince took a long gulp of whisky. "Ha, I see all; the matter is to me perfectly clear. Mr Wilde is under the impression that I will engage you to determine who is the father of the Langtry baby girl. Such an investigation was discussed by my family, and Mr Holmes' name came up. The idea was dismissed as unnecessary; both parties, Madame Langtry and my brother, agree that the child is Prince Louis'. Provision has been made for her upbringing." He shrugged, "It is a girl, thus fewer problems arise. Rumours of the family discussion may have reached Madame Langtry and disturbed her knight, Mr Wilde — that is the term, knight?"

"Knight errant is usual."

"Errant? I shall make a note." He did so with a pencil on his shirt cuff and looked up. "Do you not think that this Oscar Wilde person has exaggerated notions of concern in a matter that has already been resolved? Is he not in this affair too busy? It is unfortunate that he is not a person of rank, so that I could deal with the wretch. I must leave him to you, Mr Holmes, as you are a commoner. If you require weapons, I have a case of matched pistols and a set of rapiers in my luggage at Claridge's."

"We have decided on fisticuffs," I said. "We meet at Mr Wilde's lodgings in Tite Street tomorrow."

"Indeed? And this is a gentlemanly exercise?"

"Positively so, the rules have been endorsed by the Marquess of Queensberry."

The prince considered. "Well then, I may do you the honour of attending the event. Kindly give me the details." He again wrote on his cuff.

"And so, back to my own business. There are certain letters that I require be returned; letters not related to Madame Langtry's indisposition. These letters are in the possession of Mr Frank Miles. I intend to engage you as my agent in this matter, Mr Holmes. I should be willing to pay for the return of the correspondence, and your fee of course, in gold."

He drew two fat leather sacks from his bag and placed them on our table. They clinked in an agreeable fashion. "The matter is, as Doctor Watson suggests, delicate. The publication of the letters would embarrass a great and noble household and might have repercussions of European moment. That is all I can say, except that the correspondence is in long envelopes, on very fine paper, in a bundle tied with pink ribbon. Mr Miles holds them; he must give them up. We need not be overly nice in such affairs, *nicht wahr*?"

Holmes nodded. "I should be happy to be Your Royal Highness's agent in the matter."

Prince Alexander stood. "Your women flock to Oscar Wilde and his types with the flopping manner and poems. Bulgarian women are not attracted by these sorts. They admire a manly physique and adore fine moustaches. Also, gold lace and tight pantaloons are not amiss; for a miss — ha! I make a witticism. My brother, Louis, is a naturalised Briton; he coaches me in humour."

He slipped on his overcoat and buttoned his gloves. "I saw this *Patience*, an *opera comique* by Messrs Gilbert and Sullivan earlier in the year; it was a flabby, feminine play with no moral backbone. In the story, the ladies of the chorus prefer blushing, sunflower-holding poetical men to dragoon guards in full uniform, with cuirasses. In Sofia such a play would be booed off the stage, and the writers horse-whipped from the city."

He took up his top hat. "*HMS Pinafore*, on the other hand, was of a high tone and excellent moral character." He leaned forward conspiratorially. "I have myself Dick Deadeye played to some acclaim; in a private, court production, of course. My performance the Kaiser was kind enough to applaud with vim."

He smiled a most winning smile. "I must away — duty calls, and I am a slave to duty, ha ha. Your Mr Labouchiere stirs trouble against me in Parliament, and I have to explain myself to Mr Gladstone for my *coup d'état* against the Liberal faction in the *sabranie*." He shrugged. "I talked Tsar Alexander around to my view in Saint Petersburg last March, and in April the anarchists struck." He mimed an explosion. "I hope that your Irish dynamitards spare Mr Gladstone long enough for him to support my views in Westminster. Ha! The fiends shall not in me find so easy a target." He grinned and opened his overcoat to reveal two huge pistols in side pockets.

I saw Prince Alexander downstairs and out to his carriage. I noted the fleur-de-lyse on the door.

"I from the Prince of Wales borrowed the equipage," the prince explained. "Mine is a lightning visit, I did not even bring a horse. If I leave my capital for more than a day or two the Russians send in another dull general to take charge, or the Radicals provoke another revolution. It is vexing; I missed the Derby and almost all of Cowes."

I returned to the sitting room to find Holmes chuckling to himself. "You liked the Prince of Bulgaria," he said.

"He is an upright chap. His brother, Prince Louis, is a lieutenant in the Royal Navy." I smoothed my chin. "What do you think, Holmes, should I cultivate a beard to match my walrus moustache, a full Balaclava?"

Holmes shrugged. "They say that every man should have a hobby."

I hefted the leather bags. "Holmes, there must be close to a hundred pounds in gold here; I mean a hundred in each bag. I had no idea that this detective work paid so well. Do you usually command such sums from your clients? They seemed on the whole, if you don't mind me remarking, a rather dowdy lot."

"I am paid in guineas, Watson, or not at all."

"Of course my dear fellow. Have you any dinner plans?"

"Romano's, if you will join me?"

I grinned acceptance. "And I might remind you of our gasogene; it may take a while for the Bulgarian models to arrive and I saw a fine-looking English one in the crystal emporium for eleven and six."

I settled once more in my chair as Holmes went to the window, pulled the curtains aside and looked out on Baker Street. "What is going on, Holmes? Is Lillie Langtry at the centre of this affair? What is Mr Wilde's involvement?"

"I do not know for certain; I have five possible solutions in mind. Much will depend on whether Madame Langtry's connection is the result of a misunderstanding, as the prince suggests, or is at the centre of the case. And if not she, who?"

We took a hansom to Chelsea the following morning. Mr Miles' house was a tall, narrow, red-brick building with a pleasant, sunny aspect. Holmes and I were shown into a bright drawing room furnished with armchairs and sofas in colourful prints. Gigantic blue-and-white vases stood on the polished wooden floor in the corners of the room, and every side table had a smaller Chinese blue-and-white vase on it, each filled with an arrangement of sunflowers. The walls were covered with paintings, mostly portraits of young women that I presumed were the work of Mr Miles.

I had scarcely thought on him, when the fellow stepped in front of me, his moustache quivering with emotion.

"I am distraught," he said. "I rented a complete boxing ring from Messrs Whiteley and Co, the Universal Provider, and they promised to deliver and set it up in the Blue and White Room early this morning; I have been on tenterhooks since eight. A messenger has just arrived to say that their van is down in the Portobello Road with the ring spread across the street and looters taking rope and leatherwork. I am devastated, Doctor."

"I see," I said coldly. "And what does your handbook say about challengers who fail to secure an adequate venue?"

Mr Miles hung his head. "We forfeit."

"Let us talk to my principal." We found Holmes peering at a small green bowl that sat in a glass display case in the hall along with other dreary china. We were then led by Mr Miles into a large salon that he had set aside for the bout. The furniture had been moved to the far end of the room, and only a half-dozen almost ceiling-high Chinese vases stood against the walls.

"Plenty of room," said Holmes. "I don't expect we will dance about; Mr Wilde and I are pugilists not ballet dancers. You may demarcate the ring with rope or tape."

Mr Miles tripped off to inform his principal and Holmes whipped out his magnifying glass and began to closely examine one of the huge, blue and white vases.

"You will fight in waistcoats, Holmes."

"Eh, yes, yes."

Mr Miles returned with a large roll of pink ribbon. "This might do. It will clash with the blue and white, but we must steel ourselves. The servants are fetching hat racks as corner markers."

He leaned close to me and murmured. "Some ill-looking fellows are at the door claiming to be supporters of Mr Holmes." He consulted a note. "Master Wiggins and party."

"They are with us. Wiggins' uncle is the referee. He has considerable experience in the manly art."

The ring was set up, demarcated by the ribbon and floored with rush matting from the back corridors of the house. Both Holmes and Mr Wilde declared themselves content with the arrangements, but I objected to hat racks as too perilous, and they were replaced by high-backed dining chairs.

The room began to fill with supporters and spectators. Mr Wilde appeared from a side door in a green crushed velvet tunic, a floppy bow tie and with a huge sunflower *boutonnière*. He was a trifle taller than Holmes, I thought, and more powerfully built. He stood, holding a Champagne flute and chatting with another aesthetical gentleman whose name I had forgotten.

"Swinburne," said Holmes, turning from his examination of the vase. "Another fleshly poet."

"We had best take our places, Holmes."

More of our party arrived. A Mr Lestrade, who I knew was connected with Scotland Yard, joined us and declared that he was present in a purely personal capacity. Holmes young lieutenant, Wiggins, introduced a wizened man in a flat cap smoking a roll-your-own cigarette as his uncle Titus Marsh, the referee. He immediately took charge, writing Holmes' name on his palm with a stub of charcoal and marching across the ring to Mr Wilde.

There was a swirl of movement at the door and a gasp from Mr Miles as the Prince of Wales sauntered into the room smoking a large cigar and with Miss Sarah Bernhardt on his arm. In the group of gentlemen that followed him, I recognized Prince Alexander, and, from newspaper illustrations, Prince Louis of Battenberg, his brother. Prince Alexander took his brother by the sleeve and brought him across to Holmes' corner and made the introductions.

"Mr Holmes, I mentioned your duel to His Royal Highness at teatime yesterday, and he at once condescended to join me at the bout. I tell no secrets when I say that HRH knows of you. What of that, eh? And here is my brother on leave from his ship for Christmas, also come to cheer. Prince Albert Victor and his brother were desperate to come, but for certain reasons I had to advise against, and the Queen was firm. She does not like the boys subjected to such displays: blood etcetera and so on."

"Eddy will see plenty of blood in the Navy if the French keep up their infernal capers in Egypt," said Prince Louis with a smile.

"Are either of you gentlemen familiar with Chinese blue-and-white porcelain?" Holmes asked.

"All right gents, and lady," the referee called out in a voice that made the chandeliers tremble. "Let's get on with it. Contestants and seconds will take their places, and everyone else gets out of the way."

He flexed his arms. "And I'll tell you right here and now, any of the Fancy what accidently-on-purpose elbows a fighter, or trips him, or knees him in the whatnots (pardon my French, Miss) will answer to me. I know all the tricks, so don't even think about it. Right?"

He referred to his right palm. "In the red corner is Mr Oscar Wilde, poet, of this address." Mr Wilde stepped into the ring. The referee consulted his left palm. "In the blue corner, Mr Sherlock Holmes, Consulting Detective, of 221B Baker Street."

Holmes took off his topcoat and slipped under the ridiculous pink ribbon that demarcated the ring. He shook hands with Mr Wilde.

"Right," said Mr Marsh. "There's a three-minute limit on rounds, no grappling and wrestling; no punches to the temples, neck or below the belt; no kicking, biting or eye gouging. Got it?"

The contestants nodded.

"A man on the floor will be counted out, so no kicking or punching 'im when he's down. We ain't got no ropes so I won't go on about them. To your corners, gents. The bout will start in ten minutes so that those of the Fancy that wish to show support for their man may do so with absolute confidence courtesy of Honest Harry Wiggins, who will mingle among you; No better odds are offered nowhere else in the kingdom."

"Wait," cried Mr Miles in a shrill tone. "Is there no chance of a reconciliation, even at this late date?"

There was a long low growl from the crowd, and a voice, tinged with Hanover, damned the infernal meddler and told him to keep quiet. Mr Wilde looked across the ring at Holmes and slowly shook his head; Holmes shrugged, sat on the dining chair in his corner and lit a cigar.

I pulled up a chair in front of him and helped him with his gloves. "I say Holmes," should I not object to that enormous sun flower over Mr Wilde's breast?"

"Don't worry yourself with details, old chap. It is a fistfight, not pistols at dawn."

"He's a big, solid chap, Holmes," I replied nervously. In fact, I thought, Mr Wilde had the look of a formidable opponent, one who could absorb a great deal of punishment without flinching. Judging by the odds he was offering, Wiggins was obviously of the same opinion. He and I exchanged worried looks.

"I'm almost sure it is *Ming Chenghua*," said Holmes, puffing on his cigar.

The referee called 'Time' and Holmes and Mr Wilde stood, met at the centre of the ring, touched gloves and the fight began. Mr Wilde attacked first with a slow left hook that Holmes dodged. Holmes struck back with a straight left that missed, and he easily parried the return punch from Mr Wilde. The bout continued with each boxer offering tentative blows that the other fended off. There were murmurs and even growls and catcalls as the crowd came to the obvious conclusion that the contestant's wills were not really in the fight.

Holmes telegraphed another straight left, and as Mr Wilde backed away from the punch he tripped on a ruck in the matting, entangled himself in pink ribbon and fell out of the ring. He tried to stand and tripped again, falling against one of the huge Chinese vases that stood by the wall. It teetered, and, just as it fell, Holmes leapt out of the ring and caught it. He laid the vase gently on its side and astonished me by calling for his magnifying glass. I brought it to him and he held it in his gloved hands and glared at some Chinese signs inscribed on the base of the vase. He looked up at me and smiled. "*Ming Chenghua.*"

I helped him, Mr Wilde and several spectators heave the heavy vase upright.

"You carry a magnifying glass?" Mr Wilde asked with frown.

"You wear a sun flower?" Holmes countered with a smile.

The ring was reconstituted amid displeased murmurings in English and German from the Fancy.

Mr Wilde refreshed himself during the break with a bumper of Champagne. Holmes contented himself with a sip of water and a puff of his cigar.

The referee called time and beckoned the boxers to the centre of the ring. "Come along now gents, let's make something of the bout; we don't want to disappoint the lady do we? Fight!"

The boxers took up their stances. "Mr Holmes," said Mr Wilde coldly, "did I hear you aver that the vase I knocked over is of the *Ming Chenghua* dynasty?"

"You did."

Mr Wilde swung a tremendous left hook that Holmes just ducked away from.

"I cannot agree, Mr Holmes. It is surely *Ming Xuande* of the early fifteenth century."

Holmes feinted a left and then hit Mr Wilde with a powerful straight right to the chest that demolished his sunflower and threw him backwards.

"The mark I examined is inelegant, thick and imbalanced," said Holmes. "Common characteristics of *Ming Chenghua* porcelain."

Mr Wilde came back with a left uppercut that missed Holmes' chin by a whisker and scored across his face, bloodying his lips.

There was a roar from the crowd, and cries of 'claret!'

Holmes replied with another straight, this time left to the solar plexus. Wilde doubled up, groaned and staggered backwards.

Blood dripped from Holmes' lips onto the matting. "The *Xuande* mark was written by the famous calligrapher *Shendu*; it is simple and elegant, not at all like the blundering effort I just saw."

Mr Wilde came roaring back with a succession of short staccato blows to Holmes ribs.

"The original *Chenghua mark*

—was written by the *emperor*

—while he was *young*

—his handwriting was *immature*."

Holmes countered by stepping back and executing a right cross that, had it connected properly, would have ended the fight then and there. It skidded across Mr Wilde's head and cut his ear. Mr Miles immediately swooned and fell to the floor.

"But what of the thin potting?" Holmes cried over the roar of approval from the crowd. "And the delicate theatre scene, so typical of the period?"

The two fighters darted forward at the same time and found themselves in a clinch. "Above all, Mr Wilde," said Holmes. "What of the glaze; it is quite singular."

Mr Wilde gave Holmes a puzzled look. "There is no glaze, or hardly any."

"That," said Holmes triumphantly, "is what is singular!" He disengaged from the cinch and led Mr Wilde to the vase. He pointed with his gloved fist. "You see that the piece has a flat or matte finish. I contend that the vase was recovered from a shipwreck, and after several hundred years of emersion, the glaze is almost gone. But the reign mark on the base is bright, and newly glazed. This vase is from the *Ming Chenghua* period, re-marked in modern times as *Ming Xuande* to increase its value."

"I sold the piece to Mr Miles," cried Mr Swinburne from across the room. "You impugn my honesty!"

I looked for the referee, but he had recused himself from the bout. He sat by the window on an elegant Chippendale chair reading *The Sporting Times* and smoking another roll-your-own. I took it upon myself to call an end to the contest and declare a draw, much to the dissatisfaction of the Fancy.

Holmes and Mr Wilde were soon lost in a deep discussion on Chinese blue-and-white porcelain while I cleaned and put plasters on their cuts. The royal party let itself out without any ceremony as, under the direction of the butler, servants put the reception room to rights. After a whisky and soda with Holmes and Mr Wilde, I made a final check on Mr Miles, prostrate on an ottoman in his study, and Holmes and I took a cab home.

"Mr Wilde is meeting Mr D'Oyly Carte at the Savoy this evening to discuss his lecture tour," Holmes said with a wolfish grin as we stepped down in Baker Street. "Tonight, we strike."

I filled my pipe with tobacco from my packet, settled in my usual chair before the fire and considered our situation. A stream of visitors had appeared in our sitting room during the afternoon. They were sent off by Holmes on various errands, returning with fresh intelligence or mysterious packages. I lounged by the fire with the afternoon papers while the conspirators murmured their plans at our dining table. I had thought myself not considered for a role in whatever Holmes was cooking up, but when he had said his goodbyes and closed the door on the visitors, he turned to me.

"It is nearly five," he said. "In two hours we must be outside Mr Miles' residence waiting for him to return from his nightly promenade. Wiggins has tracked him strolling along the riverbank from six to seven accompanied by his small dog. Just before his house, he will be involved in a tussle and I shall be conducted into his study: it is the only ground-floor room with a fire and in which the gas is lit in the evening."

Holmes took a short cylinder from a package on the table and handed it to me.

"A few moments after I enter the house, I shall require the French doors of the study opened to give me air. You will fling that cylinder through the open windows and start an alarm of fire."

I examined the cylinder and saw that it was a plumber's smoke rocket, modified with percussion caps at each end.

"I am to throw this into the study and cry 'fire'. Is that all, Holmes?"

"It is, and your action is central to my strategy. Now, if you will excuse me for a moment?" He slipped into his bedroom.

I sat back in my chair and reflected on my part in Holmes' plan. The more I thought about it, the less I liked it. It seemed to me that my fellow lodger had a flair, or perhaps a weakness, for the dramatic that often led to over-complication of quite simple matters. I hefted the smoke rocket, frowned and considered my task with some trepidation; throwing a pyrotechnic into the Chelsea home of a well-known portraitist was surely felonious, however pure the motive.

The door of Holmes' bedroom opened and a Nonconformist clergyman emerged. His broad black clerical hat, his baggy trousers and general look of peering over his glasses with a benign smile were perfectly in character. I had seen Holmes in the guise of an elderly cleric on several previous occasions and I was extremely impressed by both his disguise and his performance. The stage had lost a great actor when Holmes decided on a life devoted to crime.

Holmes smiled at me. "Moral qualms, Doctor?" he said in a high, querulous voice. "You must remember that we act to protect the reputation of a noble house."

I sighed, stood and reached for my Ulster and scarf.

At fifteen minutes to the hour of seven, Holmes and I found ourselves in Tite Street. It was a clear, moonlit evening, and with the light from the gas lamps we could see perfectly well as we paced up and down in front of Mr Miles' house waiting for the return of its occupant. I was surprised that, for a small street in a quiet neighbourhood on an admittedly bright, but cold December night, the street was remarkably animated. There was a group of shabbily-dressed men smoking and laughing under a lamp post, a meat pie seller stood by his cart, a hurdy-gurdy player plied his trade and two sailors flirted with a nurse-girl near Mr Miles' gate.

"The key question is," remarked Holmes, in his character of elderly clergyman, "where are we to find the letters?"

"Where, indeed?"

"It is most unlikely that Miles carries a bundle of letters about with him."

"Where, then?"

"We shall soon see. When a man like Miles thinks that his house is on fire, his instinct is at once to rush to the thing which he values most. It is a perfectly overpowering impulse, and I have more than once taken advantage of it, and I expect to do so again. I shall inveigle my way into the house, you will cause an alarm of fire, *et voilà*!"

He smiled. "*Voilà* indeed; here, if I am not mistaken, is our quarry."

A man, heavily bundled up against the cold and with a small dog on a lead, had turned the corner into Tite Street. He strolled along the street whistling to himself an air from *HMS Pinafore*.

At a nod from Holmes, a fierce quarrel broke out between the two sailors, each of which accused the other of breaking faith with the nurse. The common loafers joined in, taking sides with one of the sailors, while the pie man was equally hot upon the other side. A blow was struck, and in an instant the gentleman with the dog was the centre of a brawling huddle of men who struck at each other with their fists and sticks.

Holmes dashed into the crowd crying for them to desist their violence, but he was struck down. At his fall, the sailors took to their heels in one direction and the loungers in the other, while the nurse attended to Holmes and the pie man and the hurdy-gurdy player helped the gentleman to his feet, dusted him off and handed him his whining dog. The gentleman bent down over Holmes. "The poor man is bleeding," he said. "He is a brave fellow. They would have had my purse and watch if it hadn't been for him. They were a gang; I am perfectly convinced they were a gang."

He stood erect. "We must carry him inside."

I smiled a wry smile; complicated though it was, Holmes' plan was working perfectly.

"Help me with him," said the gentleman. "My house is just along there, number five."

The group around the elderly clergyman stiffened and was still. Holmes picked himself up and dusted his coat. "Might I ask your name?" he asked in his petulant tone.

"I am Doctor Ernst Heppel," the gentleman with the dog replied.

"Then we need take up no more of your time, Doctor," said Holmes. He stalked across to me as the crowd dispersed and Doctor Heppel continued on his way, glancing warily about him.

I hefted my smoke bomb. Holmes shook his head. Behind him I saw a shadow move across the lighted window of Mr Miles' study.

A figure appeared beside us. "Wrong geezer, sir," said Wiggins. Holmes nodded and wiped a trickle of fake blood from his brow. He took Wiggins by the arm and murmured. "Here is what we shall have to do —"

I sighed. I was cold and my wound was playing up again. I had no time for more theatricals and parlour games.

I handed Wiggins my smoke rocket, strode across the pavement to the door of Mr Miles' house and rang a long peal on the bell. The butler answered and I requested an immediate audience with his master. The man said that Mr Miles was not at home, but I smelled tobacco smoke coming from the study door to my right. I pushed past the servant and flung open the door. Mr Miles lay on the over-stuffed ottoman in his dressing gown and tasselled fez, smoking aromatic tobacco from a hookah.

"Doctor Watson," Mr Miles said, frowning. "This a surprise. How kind of you to call" He gestured for the servant to close the door. "I am almost myself again, but I am not dressed for visitors."

"This not a social call," I said. "I require you to hand me the letters."

"I have no idea to what you are referring," Mr Miles said coolly, puffing on his pipe.

"That is a lie. You will give me the bundle of letters bound in pink tape."

Mr Miles smiled. "If I had the letters, why should I give them to you?"

"I am authorised to offer a hundred pounds for the correspondence."

"I disdain your thirteen pieces of silver."

"Gold, in fact, but if you will not return the letters for payment, you must still do so."

"Why?"

"Because, if you do not, I shall strike you on the nose with this." I held up my fist.

"You would not dare!"

"Try me."

"I shall summon a constable." He stood and moved towards the bell rope.

I wagged my finger and he stopped.

"But you know that I cannot stand the sight of blood, particularly my own. It is most ungentlemanly of you to accost me in such a decided manner."

"I am not alone," I said.

He blanched.

"Look out of the window. You will see Mr Sherlock Holmes, the pugilist, and company."

He moved to the window. "Where?"

"Eh?"

I peered out into the street through the heavy lace. "I expect that he is behind a tree, or even up it; you can never tell with

Holmes. You must take my word that he has assembled a force ready to storm the house to retrieve the correspondence."

"Oh, dear, I distinctly feel a palpitation coming on. I must have my medicine. It is in that drawer, Doctor."

I turned to the table he indicated and opened a thin drawer; it was empty. I spun around and found that Mr Miles held a heavy pistol pointed at my midriff.

"Aha, now the boot is on —"

I darted forward and snapped my stick onto his wrist; the pistol dropped and Mr Miles slumped onto an overstuffed sofa. "You have broken my wrist!"

"Nonsense, you are wriggling your fingers in an effeminate manner: kindly desist."

"I see that he will go to any lengths to retrieve the letters; but they are precious to me. They are my property. Why should I give them up? What right have you to demand them? Have you no conscience? I thought you a gentleman, Doctor."

I drew myself up and looked down my nose at the wretch. "The honour of a lady is at stake. Have you no feeling for her?"

"I do not understand." Miles put his hand to his brow. "I can take no more. The letters are in the roll top desk by the window. The key is in the lock."

I started towards the desk, stopped and frowned at Miles. "Pray oblige me by fetching them."

He nursed his arm and pouted.

I picked up the pistol hefted it. "Oblige me, Mr Miles, if you please."

"You break my heart, sir."

I was goaded beyond civility. "Rubbish, absolute rot. You do the lady no service by keeping the correspondence."

Mr Miles shook his head and collapsed once more onto the sofa. I opened the desk and retrieved a bundle of letters, bound in pink silk ribbon.

"Do you know nothing of love?" he cried as I made for the door.

I crossed the road, waved the bundle of letters at Holmes and we jumped into a hansom. Holmes was silent during our journey home.

I gave Billy my hat and coat in our hallway. "Run and get the evening newspapers, Billy. The newsagent has them bundled for us."

"Wait," said Holmes. "How much did you make in tips since you joined us?"

The boy seemed unperturbed at being addressed in his employer's voice by an elderly cleric. He counted on his fingers. "A bob from the tall gent yesterday what flung his glove about, tanner from the gent with the flower in his buttonhole this morning and a half-crown from the king of Bulgrarea; oh, and tuppence from the Doctor to put two bob on Golden Morn to win, but it didn't come up."

"Two days, and the boy has four and tuppence, Holmes!"

"Are you content with the work, young man?"

Billy grinned. "Indeed, sir."

"Then, with Doctor Watson's agreement, you may consider yourself part of the permanent establishment of 221B Baker Street, and in our employ."

I nodded and smiled at the boy. "Get along now."

"Do we expect to hear from the affronted Mr Swinburne," I asked as we ascended the stairs.

"As the challenged party, I would again get choice of weapons; I think sonnets at twenty paces; Mr Swinburne has, in my opinion, very little metrical acumen."

Holmes slipped into his room, and a few minutes later reappeared in his usual garb as an English gentleman. He strode to the fireplace, filled and lit his pipe and contemplated the bundle of letters that I laid face down on the table between us.

"What now?"

"We return the letters to the writer, or his agent in this case."

"Who is?"

"Why, your client, Prince Alexander; he will transmit them to his brother, Prince Louis of Battenberg. These are clearly the letters exchanged between the prince and Madame Langtry regarding the paternity of their love-child."

Holmes sniffed. "They are your spoils of war of course, but I would advise you to burn them unread."

"Of course I shall not read them! Theirs was a private correspondence, Holmes. I must return them to the sender."

He shook his head.

I frowned. "But why should I burn them?"

"Prince Louis would not thank you for giving them to him."

"Has that not been our goal throughout this enterprise? We aimed to avoid a European scandal involving Madame Langtry and Prince Louis."

"That was not my aim, my friend."

"I confess that I am confused, Holmes."

"The charming Prince of Bulgaria told the truth when he said that the letters were unconnected with Madame Langtry's interesting condition. His brother is involved only peripherally, advising a misguided and perhaps disturbed young friend and relation."

He leaned forward. "Without tampering with the inviolability of the correspondence that rests on our breakfast table, may we make certain deductions?"

I sniffed, but made no objections.

Holmes relit his pipe from the gas light. "The ribbon is pink silk, a traditional binding for love letters. The envelopes are larger than the usual, new and crisp, and clearly of high-quality, expensive paper. They are unstamped; indeed, 'by hand of messenger' is written across the bottom."

"Eh?" I peered down at the back of the topmost envelope and verified Holmes' observation. "If they are not addressed to Lillie Langtry, what other lady's honour is involved here, Holmes. I am at a stand. Who wrote the letters?"

Holmes frowned. "Look more carefully at the handwriting, Watson."

I did so. "It seems rather, ah—"

"Affected," Holmes offered. "Juvenile?"

"Yes, a young person's handwriting; a young man."

"You are coming along, Watson. I shall make a detective of you yet, or at least a connoisseur of blue-and-white porcelain. You will not turn the packet over and identify the addressee?"

I stiffened. "I do not feel justified in doing so, Holmes."

"Stout fellow. Might we go so far as to examine the seal?"

"I am not sure that we have that authority," I said, as Holmes whipped out his magnifying glass and subjected the broken wax to minute scrutiny.

"I believe the young man's initials, as etched in the wax, are: A, V; I conceive his other initials are C, and E for Edward."

"Albert, Victor, Christian! Eddy! The teenage son of the Prince of Wales," I exclaimed.

"Yes. Coincidently, he was sent this summer on a three-year cruise with his brother George; he is on leave for Christmas, but on a short leash."

"Aha, then the letters must show that Prince Albert Victor is the father of, ah — a certain young girl, and not as we had thought, Prince Louis. There is a need for secrecy. The boy is second in line to the throne!"

Holmes shook his head. "Mr Wilde was not concerned with Madame Langtry's reputation when he issued his challenge, but rather that of the friend with whom he boards, Mr Miles. He thought that I had been engaged to find and publish the letters, thus ruining the reputation of a young gentlemen of aristocratic distinction, and that of Mr Miles. You may recall that Mr Miles taught the young princes Art History and Composition at Osborne during the summer. The Prince of Bulgaria wanted the letters to safeguard the reputation of Prince Albert Victor, the son of his friend and confidant, the Prince of Wales. Perhaps the boy confided his infatuation with his art teacher to Prince Louis; one must remember that the prince was barely sixteen."

I blinked at Holmes as understanding dawned. I picked up the packet of letters and threw it into the fire.

As the wax seals melted and the paper crackled and burned I turned to Holmes. "Prince Albert Victor is now a midshipman and well clear of all this unseemly, Tite Street, nonsense. The Royal Navy will make a man of him."

"Yes," Holmes said looking over his newspaper with a smile. "The Navy does have an interesting reputation in that regard."

###

Trial by Jury

On a chilly morning in September, with wild gusts of wind rattling the windows and whistling down the chimney, stern-faced Inspector Lestrade was ushered into the sitting room at 221B Baker Street by our page boy, Billy; behind the inspector stood a sergeant and two constables.

Holmes looked up from his chair by the fireplace and waved his pipe in his casual manner of greeting. "Mr Lestrade, two visits in one morning. You do our house honour. Would you and your men care for coffee?"

Lestrade took out his notebook, licked the tip of a pencil and poised it in his hand. "I am afraid that this is an official visit, sir." He sniffed. "Mr Sherlock Holmes, I must ask you to accompany me to the Yard to face a charge of Wilful Murder."

Holmes raised a languid eyebrow.

"I should advise you, sir," Lestrade continued, "that anything you say may be used against you at your trial."

Holmes stood and placed his pipe on the mantel. "Then I had best say nothing."

Lestrade nodded and put away his notebook. I darted from my seat by the fire. "I say, Holmes, I must —"

My friend put a hand on my shoulder and looked me full in the face with his dark, piercing eyes. "What you must do, my dear fellow, is to promise me that you will do nothing; that you will make no move whatsoever until you hear from me. I must have that promise, Watson, and it must be a solemn oath."

I hung my head. "I do so promise."

"Good," said Holmes brightly. He turned back to Lestrade. "Whom am I alleged to have done to death?"

134

Lestrade consulted his notes. "One Charles Augustus Milverton, last evening at his home at Appledore Towers in Hampstead." He sniffed again. "I have a warrant to search these premises for the twin of this." He held up a tennis shoe.

"Very well," said Holmes, shrugging on his overcoat. "Should I pack my toothbrush?"

I sat at my desk later on that bitter day trying to comprehend the situation that Holmes and I found ourselves in, and how in a matter of mere hours our lives had been turned from comfortable and orderly (as orderly as life could be sharing rooms with Holmes) to fearful or even catastrophic. I desperately needed to talk the matter over with some competent authority. Against the spirit of my pledge, I had telegraphed Sherlock's brother, Mycroft Holmes, as soon as the door closed on the police, but I had received no reply.

I looked down at the notes that I had made of the Milverton case over the previous two weeks; I could make nothing of them. All I could think of was my friend lingering in a prison cell charged with deliberate murder.

It had been a foolhardy scheme, borne of anxiety, frustration and anger, and that it had gone horribly wrong was entirely my fault. I shook my head to clear it and stared once again at my notes, trying again to make sense of them.

Holmes and I had been out on one of our evening rambles a fortnight or so earlier, and had returned at about six o'clock to find that we had missed a caller who had left a card. Holmes read the card with disgust, and described the man whom he was obliged, in his client's interest, to meet in the most abhorrent terms. Charles Augustus Milverton was a man who lived and prospered by the misfortunes and mistakes of others: he was a master blackmailer.

He paid large sums for servants' gossip about their masters and mistresses, and especially for any indiscreet correspondence that, if released to the world, would cause a scandal and perhaps the ruin of a great family.

When the man returned later in the evening, I was surprised to find, not the slavering fiend that I had expected, but a well-dressed, middle-aged man in gold-rimmed spectacles with the benign aspect of Mr Pickwick. He blithely demanded an immense sum for the return of an imprudent correspondence between Holmes' client, a lady from fine family about to marry an earl, and a young squire. In such august circumstances, the letters, although hardly more than indiscreet, would have been enough to break off the match. Holmes acted as the lady's agent in the matter, and he had been authorised to pay as much as two thousand pounds for the return of the letters. Holmes' offer had been contemptuously refused by Milverton, and an attempt to wrest the letters from the dastard by force was foiled when he produced a pistol and slipped away.

I read my notes from that day, after Milverton left.

'Holmes sat motionless by the fire, his hands buried deep in his trouser pockets, his chin sunk upon his breast, his eyes fixed upon the glowing embers. For half an hour he was silent and still. Then, with the gesture of a man who has taken his decision, he sprang to his feet and passed into his bedroom. A little later a rakish young workman, with a goatee beard and a swagger, lit his clay pipe at the lamp before descending into the street.'

Holmes donned that workman's disguise frequently over the next few days, and I knew nothing of what he was doing except that he was occupied in some fashion in Hampstead. Then, on a wild, tempestuous evening, when the wind screamed and sleet whipped against the windows, he appeared, removed his disguise and sat before the fire, laughing in his silent inward fashion. I had noted our conversation for my casebook.

"You would not call me a marrying man, Watson?"
"No, indeed!"
"You'll be interested to hear that I'm engaged."
"My dear fellow! I congrat —"
"To Milverton's housemaid."
"Good heavens, Holmes!"
"I wanted information, Watson."
"Surely you have gone too far?"
"It was a most necessary step. I am a plumber with a rising business, Escott, by name. I have walked out with her each evening, and I have talked with her. Good heavens, those talks! However, I have got all I wanted. I know Milverton's house as I know the palm of my hand."

I looked up from my notes as I recalled the distaste with which I heard Holmes' report. I was shocked that he had deluded the young girl to the point of proposing marriage. Were there no lengths, I thought, to which my friend might go to triumph over his enemy? I turned again to my notebook.

What a splendid night it is!"
"You like this weather?"
"It suits my purpose. Watson, I mean to burgle Milverton's house to-night."

I shuddered as I recalled my absolute certainty that Holmes' actions that night would end in tragedy. And how right I was! He seemed to treat the crime he contemplated to commit as a wager or contest rather than a felony that might end his career in disgrace.

I had no choice, of course. I instantly determined that it was my duty to join Holmes in his nefarious enterprise, not only to second him, but perhaps to dissuade him from risking his reputation and perhaps his life in a foolhardy attempt if the house were close guarded or the circumstances too dangerous.

I set aside Holmes' objections to my accompanying him by the simple expedient of telling him that if he left the house without me, I would summon a constable and have him taken in charge. He was therefore forced to agree that I might be a party to his attempt to rescue the lady's correspondence from the greasy fingers of the brute, Milverton. Holmes asked me if I had a pair of silent shoes. I had noted my answer.

"I have rubber-soled tennis shoes."
"Excellent! And a mask?"
"I can make a couple out of black silk."
"I can see that you have a strong, natural turn for this sort of thing."

I looked up as the door of the sitting room opened and Mrs Hudson, eyes red-rimmed, entered with coffee and a plate of sandwiches. I had previously cancelled supper, and arranged for the messenger, Peterson, to carry a basket of cold chicken, boiled eggs and a bottle of Beaune to Scotland Yard where Holmes was incarcerated. He was allowed no visitors. I had been denied entry even when I had telegraphed Inspector Lestrade in my character as Holmes' physician.

Mrs Hudson placed a cup of aromatic coffee on the desk under my nose, and a plate of ham sandwiches with sharp mustard by the side of my notebook.

"You must keep up your strength, Doctor, you know you must. Mr Holmes will not be served by you missing supper and pining away. Peterson said the counter sergeant took the basket and promised to put it into Mr Holmes' hands directly."

I felt somewhat relieved that Holmes would at least get a square meal. I took a sip of coffee.

"And Bessie's got all the Methodies in her congregation at Mrs Arbuckle's house on the Highway praying for Mr Holmes. I wasn't sure what to think at first, but Bessie promised there'll be no hooting, crying out in tongues and waving hands about, just quiet meditation, so I gave her the evening off."

"Quite right, Mrs Hudson. Thank you for the coffee."

"Billy wants me to bake a file into a seed cake." She looked at me expectantly.

"We might come to that, Mrs Hudson, but not quite yet."

She nodded and left me.

I returned to my notes. We had entered the Milverton villa and made our way to his study. Holmes had just managed to open the safe in which the fiend kept his papers, when we realized that Milverton was still up, and that he was coming along the corridor. We hid ourselves behind some curtains.

We saw the man settle himself at his desk just in front of us, and I thought to leap out from my hiding place and knock him out, but Holmes restrained me as an outside door of the Milverton's study opened and a veiled, female figure appeared.

Their meeting was evidently arranged, for Milverton asked to see certain documents that this person had for sale that he could use to blackmail another poor devil. Instead, the figure lifted her veil and a graceful lady, of a certain age, was revealed.

"It is I," she said; "the woman whose life you have ruined."

Milverton stood and I had readied myself to deal with the wretch, when the lady took a revolver from her bosom and emptied it into Milverton's body. He slumped to the floor and she slipped away, as she had come.

I examined Milverton as Holmes raced to the interior door and locked it. He sprang to the safe and emptied bundles of documents into the fire. Only after we had ascertained that the monster was dead, and all the incriminating evidence had been disposed of, did we leave through the outside door to the garden as Milverton's domestic staff were banging at the door of the study. I followed Holmes as he raced closely chased across the back garden. Holmes leapt over a six-foot wall like a gazelle. I clambered up behind him and

'... I felt the hand of the man behind me grab at my ankle, but I kicked myself free and scrambled over a grass-strewn coping. I fell upon my face among some bushes, but Holmes had me on my feet in an instant, and together we dashed away across the huge expanse of Hampstead Heath. We had run two miles, I suppose, before Holmes at last halted and listened intently. All was absolute silence behind us. We had shaken off our pursuers and were safe.'

Or so I had thought. We had breakfasted and were smoking our morning pipes on the day after our adventure, when Inspector Lestrade, of Scotland Yard was ushered into our sitting-room in a highly excited state. Holmes asked his business, and he described a brutal murder in Hampstead. Two suspects had escaped through the grounds of the villa.

"We have their footmarks, we have their description, it's ten to one that we trace them. The first fellow was a bit too active, but the second was caught by the under-gardener, and only got away after a struggle. He was a middle-sized, strongly built man — square jaw, thick neck, moustache, a mask over his eyes."
"That's rather vague," said Sherlock Holmes. "My, it might be a description of Watson!"
"It's true," said the inspector, with amusement. "It might be a description of Watson."

Holmes had declined to act in the matter; he had no pity for the likes of Milverton. He and I saw Lestrade to the door of our sitting room. I noticed a slight twitching of the inspector's nose, and perhaps a knowing look, as he joined his sergeant in the hall and bade his farewells. We waved him away in a police carriage and I thought that we had seen the last of the inspector, at least for that day. I returned to the sitting room and lit my pipe, and after a short delay, Holmes joined me, looking pleased with himself.

The words in my notebook were blurring. I mopped my brow with my handkerchief. I had drunk more than my usual number of whiskies as I leafed through my notes, and, despite the coffee, my eyelids drooped; I made my weary way upstairs to my bedroom. As I passed the landing, I heard murmuring from the kitchen downstairs where Mrs Hudson, Billy and Bessie were still awake, doubtless discussing our problem, or perhaps in prayer.

As I lay in bed, I gulped back unmanly tears as I pictured my friend incarcerated on a capital charge; I mentally wriggled in the bands of the most solemn promise I had made. Several times during the night I leapt out of bed and paced up and down my room looking for a way to circumvent my foolish promise, offer myself at Scotland Yard as one of the burglars and tell the true story. I could not bring myself to break an oath, but I determined that if I had not heard from Holmes or his brother by noon, I would consider myself released from my pledge and I would make a full disclosure to the authorities of everything that had occurred at Appledore Towers the previous night.

I woke the next morning later than usual, my eyes gummy and with a throbbing headache. I washed and hurried downstairs to see if the early papers carried anything on Holmes' arrest. As I opened the sitting room door, I was assailed by a familiar cloud of acrid smoke, and through the fug I saw Holmes sitting at our breakfast table sipping coffee, smoking his first pipe of the day and flicking through a newspaper.

"Holmes!" I cried, blinking at him.

"There you are at last, old friend," he said. "I was about to send Billy up with a bucket of water to dash over you. I see from the level of whisky in the tantalus that you made quite an evening of it."

"Holmes," I said. "Is it really you?"

"It is indeed, after a very disagreeable night. What passes for pipe tobacco at Scotland Yard is a stain on the escutcheon of the Force. I have written a strong note to the Commissioners. Sit, enjoy this very pleasant breakfast, and I shall tell you all about it."

He stood and made for the door and, as he passed me, I grasped his hand and wrung it. He smiled, gently disengaged from me and called downstairs for more toast, hot-and-hot, and fresh eggs.

I lowered myself into my seat, still in a daze. "The thought of you in a prison cell —"

"No, no," said Holmes, sitting down and pouring coffee. "I was planted in an office and given tea and a choice of bread and dripping or digestive biscuits. Your basket of provisions was a lifesaver. I shared the wine and chicken with the desk sergeant, an affable fellow, but a teller of jokes. To compound his felony, he was also a forgetter of punch lines."

Billy came in with a rack of toast, grinning from ear to ear.

Holmes passed me the butter. "I slept on a lumpy horsehair sofa, and was given excellent tea and the morning paper by a young constable who said that he had prayed for me in company with our maid at a house off the Radcliffe Highway. It was odd, even peculiar, but quite affecting."

Holmes poured me a cup of coffee. "Lestrade joined me at seven, and we went over the evidence that he would present to his chief and to the Crown Prosecutors."

"Ha! Lestrade, that false friend."

"No, no, I rather think that we owe Inspector Lestrade a thumping dinner at the Criterion."

"Why so? He showed no compunction whatsoever about taking you in charge."

"That is because he knew that the most damning evidence in the case pointed to another."

I coloured. "The description he had from the witnesses was of me."

"And Lestrade arrested not you, but me." Holmes chuckled. "His look as he trooped into the room with his sergeant and a pair of constables was priceless. It conveyed stern admonition of course, but overlaid with sly cunning. I knew immediately that he had a plan, and I determined to go along with it."

Mrs Hudson bustled in with eggs and fresh coffee. "There's an extra egg for the Doctor, Mr Holmes, which I have to insist on as he hardly touched his sandwiches last night."

"The police search was thorough," I said as I tucked into breakfast.

Holmes nodded. "The sergeant was determined to find the other tennis shoe and make his name. But the person arrested for the crime not only did not fit the description of the witnesses, he was proved entirely innocent by his vain attempt to put on the companion of this."

He held up by the laces a scuffed tennis shoe. "I was instructed by the chief inspector to put on the mate of this shoe, and I endeavoured to do so, aided by the sergeant as valet. It was absurdly over-sized for my foot, and after several tries at walking with it flapping around my ankle, we gave up."

He smiled. "Cinderella, but the shoe did not fit. I have rather dainty feet; several people of distinction have commented on the delicacy of my feet."

The doorbell rang. I heard the door open, and slam shut again. The doorbell rang again, more vehemently, as a long shrill ring. I put my head out of the door and saw our pageboy, Billy leaning against the wall of the lobby with his arms folded, ignoring the doorbell.

"Open the door!"

"It's Inspector Lestrade, Doctor."

"Let him in out of the cold."

"But what if he's come to take Mr Holmes away again?"

"Let him in at once."

The boy pouted and slouched to the door.

A few moments later Inspector Lestrade joined us in the sitting room muttering about young jackanapes not minding their elders.

"Coffee, Inspector?"

"Thank you, Mr Holmes. I am chilled from standing in the doorway —"

Holmes held up the tennis shoe. "I was describing our little fairy tale to Watson. My regular shoe and the twin of this glass slipper were examined and compared. The tennis shoe clearly belonged to a person with large feet — army issue feet."

"I say, Holmes —"

Holmes smiled. "The under-gardener's description of the felon: middle-sized, strongly built, square jaw, thick neck and moustache also did not fit me. And I was released."

"Thank goodness for that," I said. "I had some notion that I had lost the shoe, but in the excitement I did not consider the loss important."

"It was found by a under gardener at Appledore Towers early this morning as he was re-enacting his chase of the villains before the police. It was sent to the Yard by messenger, arriving just as Mr Lestrade and his sergeant returned from their visit to us."

Lestrade smiled. "My sergeant started like a pointer when he saw the shoe. He said that he'd seen the other one when we visited 221B Baker Street. I was forced to confirm that I had seen a similar shoe in the hall stand."

Holmes refilled his pipe. "My reluctance to take up the case had piqued Lestrade's interest. His nose led him to scrutinise the contents of the hall stand on which our boots and shoes are stored as he left us for the Yard. You had automatically dropped the shoe on the stand as we returned home from our misadventure in Hampstead. It fell behind my Wellington boots and was missed by Mrs Hudson's eagle eye, but it did not escape Inspector Lestrade's nose. And he saw that his sergeant had followed his gaze and also noticed the shoe."

"I wonder why I did not just fling it into a bush as I did the mask," I said.

"You were under a certain stress, and we were, quite literally, on the run."

Lestrade stood and took out his notebook. "Mr Holmes has explained what happened at Appledore Towers, but he refuses to give me a description of the lady who fired the fatal shots. Will you do so, Doctor?"

"I will not."

Lestrade nodded and closed his notebook. "I shall leave you then, gentlemen. I fear this will have to be one of our failures." He nodded at the rubber-soled shoe. "I'd stick that in the furnace, was I you."

Holmes lit his pipe as Billy showed Lestrade to the door. "I saw Lestrade's interest. As soon as the inspector left with his sergeant, I retrieved the shoe and had Billy put it in his hideaway. It could not go in the rubbish, as that was sure to be searched if the police returned; it could not be burned in case the searchers were alerted by the smell of burning rubber. And I did not want you or Mrs Hudson involved. You might be suspected and arrested as an accomplice. She cannot lie; it is against her Scottish nature. Billy is an accomplished prevaricator."

"Hideaway?"

"All boys have hideaways where they keep their contraband; in Billy's case, he hides his cigarettes and photographs of Miss Marie Lloyd, the music hall artiste with whom he is currently infatuated, behind a couple of loose bricks in the cupboard under the stairs. He was reluctant to take the shoe at first, thinking it, with some supporting evidence, damp and slightly odorous, but I prevailed upon his loyal nature; I also threatened to tell Mrs Hudson about a certain matter of a half-bowl of cherries that feloniously evaporated while on the sill of the kitchen window last Sunday."

Holmes folded himself into his armchair in front of the fire.

"I was released on my own recognisance by the chief inspector this morning, but, as that gentleman is reluctant to take responsibility for dismissing what would obviously be a sensational case, I must return at three o'clock today for a final verdict from the Director of Public Prosecutions. He will, according to Lestrade, wish me good day and apologise for any inconvenience."

Billy reappeared at our sitting-room door and asked if we required anything.

"Thank you, Billy, no," I answered. "But, it seems that I owe you a debt, young man. If there is anything —"

The boy beamed and Holmes answered my question. "Miss Lloyd is on at the Alhambra, Watson. Half a crown would suffice; any more would be wasted on roses and chocolates, with which I am certain the lady is amply provided."

I slipped a half-sovereign from my waistcoat pocket. Billy took it and scampered away.

Holmes chuckled. "Bribing a witness, Doctor Watson: another hideous crime."

I reddened. "I will accompany you to Scotland Yard, Holmes."

"No, no, you may not come; the witnesses to the escape of the two men will be present. Your moustache has attained a well-oiled lustre that, once viewed, is hard to forget; it is a topiary." He saw my dogged look and sighed. "Very well, you may sit in a cab, out of sight, and, after the hearing, I will treat you to a glass of Bordeaux at the Criterion."

Holmes waved his pipe stem. "The lady overindulged herself, Watson. A single shot to the head, and a complaisant coroner would have ruled that the hound Milverton committed self-murder in a welter of remorse. But five bullets in the chest would stretch the credulity of even a London jury."

Holmes and I set off for Scotland Yard after luncheon; he was in high spirits, but I was still very uncomfortable with the idea that he was in danger, while all the evidence pointed to me. He was gone but a few minutes. He jumped up into the cab looking troubled.

"Holmes?"

"Oh, charges dismissed. That is the end of the Milverton matter."

"And?"

"A pretty kettle of fish, my dear fellow. The Milverton housemaid, Aggie, was in the room with the other witnesses to our getaway from Appledore Towers; she recognized me instantly. As soon as the affable gentleman from the DPP's office dismissed the case, she sidled up to me and said that the plumbing business must be going main well if Ernie Escott could dress as a toff and take rooms in Baker Street."

"You proposed marriage, Holmes."

"Mmm? Yes, I believe I did, to a certain degree."

"It is not something that admits of degrees."

"I bow to your expertise in the matter."

"Holmes."

He took my arm. "I am sorry, my dear friend; I apologise unreservedly. I have to admit that I had completely forgotten about the girl. She did not occur to me. It is vexing."

I frowned. "If she testifies that you were going about disguised in the neighbourhood of Milverton's villa days before the killing, that must force the police to reopen the case against you."

"I wonder what young Aggie will do," Holmes mused. "She is gullible, but no fool. What will be her next move?"

"Blackmail?"

"It is possible."

The cabby opened his hatch and gave us a quizzical look. "You gents going anywhere or are you putting down roots?"

I checked my watch. "We must get legal advice. Yes, we have enough time, but there is not a moment to lose. Pall Mall, Cabby, as quick as you like."

Our cab dropped us in Pall Mall outside the door of the Diogenes Club. We stepped into the hall and I wrote a note and gave it to the dusty porter. He disappeared into the Reading Room and a few minutes later Mycroft Holmes came through the heavy glass doors, held out his hand to me and ushered us into the Strangers' Room where we could talk freely.

"How are you, Doctor? My dear Sherlock, I had expected to see you in the Clink chained to an iron ball when next we met. I understand that you rid the world of the repulsive Milverton."

"Not quite."

Holmes told his brother of our adventures at Appledore Towers, and of the lady who had killed the fiend.

"We are well rid of that fellow, Sherlock. I thought you had done the deed. I was going to send my congratulations, discreetly, of course. A number of fellow members of the Diogenes Club nodded to me this morning in a decided manner; word is getting around. Tea?"

He pulled a bell rope by the fireplace. "I received your telegram, Doctor, only this morning. It arrived last evening, but the stupid boy who infests the building in which I lodge put it under the door of my neighbour, newly returned from the Khyber. When I read your message, I contacted the Home Office and was assured that all was well and Sherlock was not to be charged; I sent you a note to that effect which is probably waiting for you at your lodgings."

Mycroft offered cigars and turned to his brother as he lit his. "What of the girl, Sherlock? The house is in Hampstead; is she a cream-and-strawberries milkmaid?"

"Originally from Eastbourne," Holmes answered.

"Ah, a knowing minx, then? No blushing violet?"

Holmes shrugged. "I did not take a great deal of notice. I was in the character of a raffish young tradesman. I allowed my character some latitude."

"Altogether too much it seems. Really, Sherlock, I thought you too fly for this sort of nonsense. I suppose we may face an action for breach of promise."

I stood. "It is entirely my fault —"

Mycroft waved me back into my chair. "It is abundantly clear that one of the most powerful causes of the shyness of men in matters matrimonial is the frequency of breach of promise prosecutions. Your wavering, undecided, fastidious bachelor is a great newspaper reader and devours breach of promise cases; after reading that Miss Tonks has obtained so many hundred pounds damages against her fiancé, he concludes that the best salve for a wounded heart is gold. And thus, for fear of being trapped into committing himself, he avoids the society of women and eventually settles down into old bachelorhood."

"So saith a crusty old bachelor," said Holmes. "I read your letter to *The Times* on the matter at the time of publication."

"I can assure you that my views carry weight with the government," Mycroft answered with a slight pout. "And with the judiciary."

A knock and the door opened to a servant with a tray of tea and cakes.

"Let me see," said Mycroft, counting on his fingers. "We have nine possibles at the Club, all senior barristers with civil court experience. We have a plethora of judges, of course, those most self-important and un-clubbable of men."

He poured the tea. "First, let us find a solicitor. They do not, on the whole, enjoy the benefits of the Diogenes, they are talkative, busy fellows, but we have one or two. We will engage Mr Pertwee; he is malleable. And he may brief Sir Vandissart Bullimore, if he is available."

"Ahem, gentlemen," I began, waiting until the servant had left before I continued. "There is one other possibility we must explore."

Holmes and Mycroft looked expectantly at me.

"Pay the girl off."

The brothers exchanged pitying looks. "Come, Doctor, you should know the Holmes family motto," Mycroft admonished me. "Permanence, perseverance and persistence in spite of all obstacles, discouragements, and impossibilities."

"It is this," Holmes continued, "that distinguishes the strong soul from the weak."

I sipped my tea and said nothing as the strong-souled brothers planned their forensic stratagems.

Holmes and I arrived back in Baker Street after a pleasant dinner at the Criterion. We stepped out of the cab onto the crowded pavement outside 221B.

A short man in a bowler pushed through the throng.

"Mr Sherlock Holmes, sir?"

"I am."

"Then this is for you, sir." He handed Holmes a roll of paper, tipped his hat and disappeared into the crowd.

We made our way inside and up to our sitting room where Holmes passed me the roll of paper and I broke the seal. "It is a summons Holmes! You are to be subpoenaed in the matter of Butterworth v Holmes (alias Escott) for breach of promise to marry Agatha Butterworth, housemaid, previously residing at Appledore Towers in Hampstead."

Holmes shrugged. "Now we know."

I watched Holmes adjust his cravat in the sitting room mirror on the morning of his trial. "No, no, Watson, you cannot appear as a character witness for me. You would be instantly recognized as one of the felons who raided the home of the vile Milverton. Your glorious walrus moustache and fine military bearing give you away, my friend."

"Very well," I agreed, most reluctantly. "Call me when you are ready to go, and I will say my goodbyes."

Holmes smiled and nodded.

I stomped upstairs to my bedroom and stood at the wash basin, girding my loins. I blinked at my reflection, sighed a huge sigh and lathered my face.

I opened the door of the sitting room to find Holmes still at the mirror. He looked up and spun around. "Watson — is it you?"

"It is." I watched in the mirror as the strange person who was now me rubbed the place where my walrus moustache, nurtured for over fifteen years and anointed twice daily with Rowland's Macassar Oil, had been.

"My dear, dear fellow; I grieve with you." Holmes strode across the room and grasped my hand. "Greater love hath no man than this: that he shave off his moustache for a friend. I am greatly moved, old fellow."

He wrung my hand in a manly fashion, and we filled our pipes, lit them and puffed hard to conceal our emotions.

Holmes put on his overcoat. "You might care to shuffle into the courtroom, Watson, as if borne down by circumstance. It might go some way to concealing your erect military bearing."

Inspector Lestrade waited for us in the colonnade outside the court building. He sniffed, glanced at my upper lip and shook his head. "A baddish business, gentlemen."

Holmes nodded as we were joined by Mycroft Holmes and our solicitor, Mr Pertwee.

Mr Pertwee peered anxiously at Holmes over his spectacles. "Might I pray once more that you retain a barrister, Mr Holmes? I speak with your very best interests in mind. Sir Vandissart Bullimore appears for the plaintiff; he is pitiless in cross examination."

"You will not move him," said Mycroft. "He ached to play the part of Portia in *The Merchant of Venice* when we were at school, and threw a tantrum when a prettier boy got the role. He would line up his wooden soldiers, grip his jacket lapels and orate to them. He has always wanted to address a British jury."

"At least I did not wear a mop on my head while playing a judge," said Holmes tartly.

"That is a vile calumny," cried Mycroft.

I checked my watch. "Gentlemen, we must take our places."

We stood as the judge, Baron Kingsford Cresswell entered the surprisingly cramped courtroom and the usher called for silence. The judge settled himself, and Mycroft, Mr Pertwee and I took our places in the row of chairs behind Holmes' table as the usher requested those with business in the court to identify themselves.

The prosecutor, in his gown and wig, and with a monocle in his left eye, stood and bowed to the judge. "I am Sir Vandissart Bullimore, Your Honour. I appear for the plaintiff."

Holmes stood. "My name is Sherlock Holmes. I am a consulting detective. I appear for myself."

The judge glared at Holmes. "I have heard your name, Mr Sherlock Holmes, and I am aware of your profession, one of which I by no means approve."

"In that, My Lord, you will find yourself in agreement with every criminal in the country," Holmes replied. "I trust that Your Lordship has fully recovered from your exertions in Queensway?"

"Eh? What did the fellow say? What was that?"

"A good start," Mycroft murmured, glancing at his watch. "Forty seconds into the trial and Sherlock has already alienated the judge's affection."

I studied the jury, all male of course and judging by their clothing and deportment, men of the middle class; they huddled tightly, and probably uncomfortably, in two benches to the right of the judge. They listened as Sir Vandissart outlined the case against Holmes and stirred with interest as he called his first witness.

A young girl, dressed in a flowing wedding dress, tiara and veil slipped across the courtroom and into the witness box. At a gesture from the usher she folded her veil over her hair and revealed a pale, pretty face framed with curly blonde hair.

Sir Vandissart addressed her in avuncular tones. "Your name is Agatha Butterworth, and you work as a housemaid at Appledore Towers in Hampstead?"

"No, Your Honour."

"Eh? I am not His Honour, that is the judge. And kindly address your answers to the jury."

The judge smiled down at Miss Butterworth, his eyes gleaming, and pointed to the two rows of men at benches opposite. They looked on Miss Butterworth's comely features with a worrying intensity of interest.

"You are Miss Butterworth?" said Sir Vandissart in a puzzled tone.

She directed a brilliant smile at the judge. "I am."

"You work at Appledore Towers?"

She pouted. "Not any more. My employer, Mr Milverton, was cruelly murdered and I have lost my position; I am out in the street without a character." She pulled a large frilly handkerchief from her bosom and wiped a tear from her eye.

"I am sorry to hear that, Miss Butterworth," said the judge, shaking his head. The jury murmured agreement and glared at Holmes with stern disapprobation. Mr Pertwee and I exchanged worried looks, but Holmes seemed serenely unaffected.

"Do you know the person seated over there?" Sir Vandissart asked, pointing an accusing finger at Holmes.

"Yes, he is Ernie Escott, who plighted his troth to me last Sunday week in poor Mr Milverton's vegetable garden. My father advanced a sum, and I went the very next day to Whiteley's and ordered my dress, then to Maples and picked out a suite of furniture for — oh, I swoon," she cried, and promptly did. Two of her supporters, servants from Milverton's residence, helped her from the courtroom. Holmes waived his right to cross-examine. I stood and offered my medical services, and the judge assented.

I administered smelling salts, and prescribed a small brandy from the pub across the road as a restorative, then left Miss Butterworth in an ante room. When I returned to the courtroom, the first witness from Appledore Towers and its environs was attesting to Holmes' identity as Ernest Escott, plumber, and to his 'walking out' with Miss Butterworth. The under gardener, who I knew from Holmes was the his rival in the courtship of the young lady, was on the stand.

"This Escott, the man sat there sir, bold as brass, walked out with my Aggie — Miss Butterworth — for nigh on a fortnight.

It was the talk of the house, sir, below stairs. He passed afore me, sir, though he had no right of way; he bore my love away. I was taken aback."

The judge peered over his *pince-nez*. "What's your witness talking about, Bullimore?"

"I believe the witness was a mariner before he took up under-gardening. He is speaking in nautical terms."

"Adjure him to desist."

Sir Vandissart bowed and, after Holmes again failed to cross examine, dismissed the witness. "I understand that Mr Holmes wishes to take the stand," he told the judge with a wolfish grin.

Holmes entered the witness box and faced the prosecutor with a slightly amused expression on his face. I knew that he had very little time for legal niceties, or for most practitioners of the law; I prayed that he would remain temperate.

Having established Holmes' identity, and with some growls from the judge, his profession, Sir Vandissart began his examination.

"Is it true that, in the common parlance, you 'walked out' with Miss Butterworth?"

"It is."

"You were attracted to her?"

Holmes looked across the courtroom at the plaintiff and considered. "It is of the first importance not to allow your judgment to be biased by personal qualities. Emotional qualities are antagonistic to clear reasoning. I assure you that the most winning woman I ever knew was hanged for poisoning three little children for their insurance-money. Miss Butterworth's physical attractions, although considerable by all reports, were not a factor in my interest in her."

Sir Vandissart blinked at Holmes. "You admit that you were interested in Miss Butterworth?"

"I do."

"You admit that you paid her a certain class of attention?"

"That is so."

"You went for walks together?"

"We did."

The prosecutor leered at Holmes. "*Long* walks?"

Holmes frowned and addressed the judge. "Might I have some guidance, Your Lordship, as to what length of walk, in furlongs perhaps, might be considered long in the village of Hampstead?"

"Whether short or long," Sir Vandissart said with a smirk, you walked. "What did you talk of during these *walks*?"

"Bees," said Holmes.

A shock went around the court; even the prosecutor seemed amazed. "Am I to understand, Mr Holmes that you spoke with this innocent young lady of the matters related to the birds and the —"

"Bees: apiary, the keeping of honey bees. Miss Butterworth's father is a master beekeeper at the family residence in Sussex. The young lady is a fountain of knowledge on the subject."

Holmes smiled at Miss Butterworth and she permitted herself a dainty pout in return.

"We also talked of marriage; I have nothing in particular against marriage, indeed I have heard reports of polygamy, as practised by the Mormon sect in Utah, suggesting that their community of men married to multiple wives flourishes; it is an interesting experiment."

Sir Vandissart was not distracted; he homed in on the crux of the matter. "Is it possible," he asked, "that Miss Butterworth construed your discussions as a prelude to an offer of marriage?"

The court went deathly still.

"It is more than possible; it is probable. You are too timid in drawing your inferences, Sir Vandissart. Why do you not you ask me whether I proposed marriage to Aggie?"

Sir Vandissart narrowed his eyes. "Did you propose marriage to Miss Butterworth?"

"I did."

Holmes' admission was met with a roar of disapproval from the spectators. The jurymen glared at him; one stood and waved his fist. The usher banged his stave on the floor and restored order.

"Were you at that time in disguise and using a false name?" Sir Vandissart asked over the hub-bub.

"I was. I sailed under false colours, as my nautical rival would have it; it was a *ruse de guerre*."

The judge's quill paused. "A what?"

"A trick to confound the enemy," Sir Vandissart explained and the judge's quill moved again.

"Why were you dressed as a common tradesman, and using a false name?" Sir Vandissart asked.

"I cannot, in conscience, answer that. I was pursuing a case, a matter of great delicacy not germane to this inquiry."

"I am afraid that I must press you, Mr Holmes. It is for His Honour and the jury to decide what is relevant and what irrelevant."

"I decline to answer; the matter concerns the good name of a lady."

The judge erupted. "Another lady? A different lady to Miss Butterworth?"

"She is."

The judge scribbled furiously in his notebook.

"You refuse to answer the question," said Sir Vandissart. "The jury must therefore draw their own conclusions; the circumstances are suspicious, are they not?"

"Circumstantial evidence is a very tricky thing," Holmes answered thoughtfully. "It may seem to point very straight to one thing, but if you shift your own point of view a little, you may find it pointing in an equally uncompromising manner to something entirely different."

He pursed his lips. "And yet, there is nothing more deceptive than an obvious fact."

Sir Vandissart blinked at Holmes through his monocle. "I conclude the case for the plaintiff, My Lord."

The judge declared a break for luncheon.

Mr Pertwee nodded to me, and we slipped out of the courtroom into the lobby.

"What do you think?" I asked.

Mr Pertwee shook his head. "English jurymen do love a comely plaintiff." He chuckled. "The wedding dress was typical Sir Vandissart: he is a sly dog. And jurors with marriageable daughters will not like the element of disguise and the false name that Mr Holmes assumed. Indeed, I fear that these unusual elements in the tale will have a profound effect on the jury. He admits that he promised marriage; it is now merely a question of to what precise degree (in bright golden sovereigns) the jury will find Mr Holmes a callous, heartless fiend. There is a delicate sliding-scale for defendants in such cases. A reluctant bridegroom, well-made and well-to-do, will pay heavily for the damage he has done to a pretty, vulnerable young thing like Aggie. We must urge your friend to call character witnesses from the list I have compiled. Mr Holmes spoke of a *ruse de guerre*; we may be able to muddy the false-name waters by a reference to the Nation's security (unmasking French conspirators, for choice). The Home Secretary is willing to speak on Mr Holmes' behalf, as are half the earls in the Red Book and much of the nobility in the *Almanach de Gotha*."

Our side: Holmes, Mycroft, Mr Pertwee and I gathered in a corner of the bar of a pub across the street from the court. "I say, Holmes," I asked, "are you quite well?"

Mr Pertwee was more direct. "You will need some very convincing character witnesses if you are not to face an award of massive damages, Mr Holmes. I have never seen a less sympathetic jury. And if I may say so, your own attitude —"

Holmes waved Mr Pertwee's objection away. "I intend to call two character witnesses."

"I have a list here of persons of august rank furnished by your brother and headed by no less than —"

Holmes shook his head. "No, no. People who know me in my private capacity."

"Very well, if they are persons of substance."

"Don't worry, Mr Pertwee, I have made the arrangements."

"This is all rather disorderly, Mr Holmes," said Mr Pertwee in a heavy tone. "Unorthodoxy does not go down well with your average British jury."

Holmes smiled a thin smile.

"You don't need Bessie, do you, Holmes?" I asked to lighten the mood. "She's in a house on the Highway praying for your elevation to sainthood."

"Ah," said Holmes, looking behind my back, "here is my first witness."

I turned and immediately recognized Harry Wiggins, the young leader of the band of street Arabs that Holmes employed to track suspects and run errands across London. He wore a loud check suit and a wide-awake hat, and he looked the very image of the teenage criminal and racing tout that I knew him to be.

"Afternoon, gents." He waggled his finger at Holmes. "Tut, tut, Mr Holmes. I never thought you such a flat as to get caught with a marriage promise to a floosy: a housemaid, sir, and in

Hampstead, tsk tsk. I trust there is no paper in the case, no *billets-doo* as the *Monsieurs* say?"

Holmes shook his head and grinned. "What do you have?"

"Not much on the judge that we don't know already, Mr Holmes. Baron Cresswell is a member of the Diogenes Club and has a kept woman in Queensway that he visits each evening at five. He has three children, one by his first wife and then two by his second. His middle son is a bad gambler, and his youngest a main good liar."

He held out a sheet of paper and Holmes studied it. "Oh yes, we have the judge on — well, let's just say the judge is no saint, and Sir Vandissart has a surprisingly lively social life for a man who wears such a decided monocle."

Wiggins grinned.

"And Aggie and the under-gardener —" Holmes looked up. "But I see Watson looking at me with a furrowed brow; do not concern yourself, old chap. These exertions were merely to clear the air; to determine whether the parties have other agendas. I do not intend to act on the knowledge of the judge's weaknesses, or the prosecutor's iniquities or even the plaintiff's affinities. The case will stand on its own merits, or not at all."

We filed back into court, and Holmes called Wiggins to the stand. I cringed inwardly as I saw the impression that this confident young scoundrel made on the judge and jury.

"You are Master Harry Wiggins, currently working as a costermonger's assistant at the Lower Marsh in Lambeth."

"I am."

"Have you been in court before?"

He laughed. "Have I ever; mostly in the dock same as you are now, Mr Holmes, but at the Assizes."

"On what charges?"

"Dipping mostly, a bit of slum paper, duff fivers, the parcel dodge, fencing — all the usual lays."

The judge slapped down his quill. "What's the fellow talking about, Bullimore?"

"Perhaps I can help, Your Honour?" Holmes offered. "Mr Wiggins is a professional criminal with convictions for pickpocketing, fraud, counterfeiting, misrepresentation and receiving stolen goods."

Wiggins grinned. "I got off that last one, sir."

"Very well. How would you characterise your relationship with me?" Holmes asked.

"I hope that I may count myself an acquaintance and business partner, sir, without presuming above my station."

"Detail our business relationship, if you would?"

"I fix up any slum paper as is wanted — false identification and so on, keep an eye on rum geezers what are in whatever case we're on; general work, you might call it. I also put the Doctor's bets on the gee-gees."

"You have a band of accomplices in these nefarious deeds?" Holmes asked.

"They wasn't let in, on account of shoes."

"Shoes?" asked the judge. "The court makes no sartorial provisions in the matter of shoes."

Holmes smiled at him. "He means not having them, Your Honour. Mr Wiggins' companions are ragged street Arabs."

The judge shook his head and returned to his notebook,

"You visit me at my lodgings, at all hours, with your ragged company?" Holmes asked Wiggins.

"We do, and very welcoming you are too, sir."

I distinctly heard the judge mutter 'Fagin' under his breath.

"Who do I know? Who do I do business with?" Holmes continued.

"There isn't a villain in London doesn't know you, sir. All the top men have had dealings with Mr Sherlock Holmes."

"Thank you, Wiggins." Holmes looked across to the prosecution bench.

"Don't mind me," said Sir Vandissart, with a smile. "No questions. We're all very happy on this side."

"I call Doctor John Watson," said Holmes.

I started and looked about me.

"Doctor?"

I slowly rose and made my way across the court to the witness box. Holmes established my identity, made me detail my military service, confirm that I was a general practitioner and attest that I shared lodgings with him at 221B Baker Street.

"When did you first meet me, Doctor?"

"In 1881; I was at a loose end in London, looking for lodgings. I met a friend who knew you. He suggested that we meet you at the Laboratory at St Bartholomew's Hospital."

"Did your old friend say anything about me?"

"He said that you had a passion for exact knowledge."

"Did he mention anything about my habits in the Laboratory, particularly the dissecting room?"

I shifted my feet and blinked at Holmes. "I'm not sure that I recall —"

"Come now, Doctor, you are on oath. I must press you for a truthful answer."

I took stern command of my senses. "He said that you had a habit of beating the cadavers in the dissecting room with a club. You said that it was to determine the amount of bruising that may occur after death."

A murmur of disapprobation went around the courtroom. The usher looked at Holmes with distaste and the judge stirred. "Are you quite happy with this line of questioning Sir Vandissart? Do you feel that it is germane to the matter at hand?"

"I am content to let Mr Holmes have the greatest freedom in presenting his evidence, Your Honour," said Sir Vandissart, bobbing up and smiling.

The judge slapped down his pen. "Very well then."

"Do I read your mind?" Holmes asked.

"You do. At least, that is what I call your feats of deduction."

"Eh? What did the fellow say?" asked the judge.

"Doctor Watson admitted that I can read his mind, Your Honour," said Holmes.

I reddened as a clerk tittered, the jurymen nudged each other and laughter could be heard from the gallery.

"Are you on the boards?" asked the judge with a judicial leer. "I've not seen you at the Alhambra. Perhaps, with Bullimore's indulgence, we might have a demonstration of your mind-reading prowess?"

The court laughed dutifully.

Holmes smiled a tight smile. "I do not read minds, Your Honour; I deduce facts from evidence." He looked across to the prosecution bench and put his finger to his lip in a characteristic gesture. "It is clear, for example, that Sir Vandissart Bullimore is a mason, but that he does not attend his lodge regularly. He may be expecting a promotion in his profession. Despite that expectation, he has recently embraced a more frugal style of life. As Your Lordship may agree, the cost of upkeep for more than one household might stretch the finances even of a successful QC."

Sir Vandissart's monocle dropped on its ribbon and he gaped at Holmes. "Your Honour, I, I —"

Holmes turned to me. "Doctor?"

I regarded Sir Vandissart closely as I applied Holmes' method of scientific deduction. "Sir Vandissart has a masonic pendant on the end of his watch chain," I said. "Silver, but dull and tarnished; I imagine it would be polished before masonic meetings. His wig is tattered and he has not chosen to replace it; perhaps he expects a promotion into a position that requires a different style of wig. His suit is of the very highest quality, but his left shoe has been very recently resoled, suggesting a need for economy."

The judge glared at Sir Vandissart and banged his gavel. "Continue your examination of this Witness, Mr Holmes. And keep to the matter at hand."

Holmes bowed and turned back to me. "We have shared rooms for many years now, have we not, Doctor?"

"We have. And I hope that we —"

"Am I a congenial companion? Remember, you are on oath."

I considered. "You can be most congenial, at times; less so in the morning, perhaps, and when you do not have a case. It is quite understandable given your great —"

"Am I something of a know-it-all, an Admirable Crichton? Do I display my esoteric knowledge in a boastful manner, and drop the names of important people, particularly European monarchs, into our conversation?"

"You do. And you do tend to —"

"— finish other people's sentences?"

I nodded.

"What of my general knowledge?"

I thought for a moment. "You said that a man should possess all knowledge which is likely to be useful to him in his work, and this you have endeavoured to do. Other knowledge, you maintain, is superfluous." I saw a smile flit across Holmes' face as he realised that I remembered his recent remarks on the subject.

"Are there obvious areas of knowledge in which I am deficient, Doctor?"

"You did not know that the earth revolved around the sun and you said that you had never heard of Mr Thomas Carlyle."

The judge started and leaned forward. "He had not heard of Carlyle? Everyone knows Carlyle. He was a neighbour of mine in Chelsea. Tut, tut, Mr Holmes. But, wait, are we not straying once again from the matter at hand?"

"We on the plaintiff's side are perfectly content, Your Honour," said Sir Vandissart with a warm smile at Holmes.

The judge turned to Holmes. "I should warn you, sir, that you are making no positive impression on this court with the line of questioning that you are pursuing. If I thought that you were indulging in some sort of ironical display, or twisted self-promotion, I would not be lenient."

"My Lord," said Holmes in a pious tone. "I am a humble seeker after truth. I believe this court, and the young lady on the other side of the chamber, deserve to know with whom they are dealing; I reveal myself, as did Oliver Cromwell, warts and all."

The judge muttered to himself again, and I clearly heard 'bother Oliver Cromwell'.

"I smoke several pipes per day?" Holmes asked me.

I nodded warily. "As do I"

"What is the most disagreeable form of tobacco that I smoke in our sitting room?"

I grimaced. "Your morning pipe, of course. You gather the dottles left over from the previous day's smoking, and stuff them into your first pipe of the morning."

"It is acrid?"

"Poisonous."

"Have you informed me of your dislike for this practice?"

"On numerous occasions."

"And yet I continue to smoke that repellent mixture with no thought at all for your comfort."

'You sometimes open the window, especially if it's blowing hard and raining cats and dogs. Ha ha." I looked around, but no-one else in the courtroom seemed to share my mirth.

The judge had been regarding Holmes in frank incredulity. "The fellow does what?"

Holmes smiled up at him. "Doctor Watson attests that I leave the burned plug of tobacco from each pipe of yesterday on the fire grate, and that I smoke them again in my first pipe of today."

"Extraordinary behaviour," said the judge. He turned to the prosecutor. "What club would accept such a person, Bullimore? Is the wretch even in Society? Have you no objection to these sordid revelations?"

Sir Vandissart stood and bowed to the judge and to Holmes. "Do not mind me at all, Mr Holmes." He sat, glanced at the jury and exchanged a satisfied look with his junior.

"You consider smoking yesterday's dottles a bad habit, Doctor?" Holmes asked me.

"It is a foul habit, Holmes. Mrs Hudson is particularly —"

"Hearsay Doctor, I must beg you to refrain from indulging in hearsay."

I reddened and said nothing.

Holmes smiled. "Do I maintain a cheery, sportive disposition?"

I considered. "When you are engaged in a challenging case, yes."

"And when I am, shall we say, between cases?"

"You can be trying at times. You have a tendency to melancholia."

"I play the violin?"

"You can play, and very well. During your black periods you persuade the instrument to emit dark and dreary chords and shrieks, ha ha." Again, the court was not disposed to chuckle with me. "During these black periods you do not eat, or at least eat properly. As your physician as well as your friend, I have attempted to persuade you to take healthy exercise, eat and sleep regularly and limit your intake of —"

"Cocaine?"

"I was going to say tobacco," I answered coldly.

"I am sorry, Doctor, I interrupted you again. But I do indulge in cocaine, injected as a seven-per-cent solution, do I not?"

I sniffed. "Much less than before."

"Do I practise pistol shooting in the sitting room?"

"You have done, in a patriotic way; the pockmarks in the wall are nearly faded."

The judge looked up from his notes. "Mr Holmes shot holes in your sitting room wall, Doctor?"

I nodded. "VR, after our own dear queen, in bullet pocks, with a revolver."

The judge shook his head and returned to his notes.

"You mentioned beating cadavers at Barts," Holmes said. "Do I also engage in chemical experiments?"

"You do."

"Where?"

"In the living room. You have set up a laboratory bench against one wall."

"This is the room in which we eat, converse, read the newspapers and smoke our pipes?"

"It is."

"Is that not discommoding for you?"

"For me and the whole household, Holmes. Mrs Hudson, Bessie and Billy live in mortal fear of the concoctions you mix at your bench." I turned to the judge. "Can you imagine, My Lord, taking tea in the afternoon amid the reek of carbolic acid or even more volatile and dangerous substances? I have remonstrated with Holmes on many occasions, but there is always the cry that a man's life hangs on the result of this experiment, that so-and-so will face the noose if the litmus turns red." I turned back to Holmes. "It is not good enough, old man. Why not long ago you concocted a deadly poison from powdered rosary beads and administered it to General Gordon."

The judge roused himself again. "What are you saying, I do not understand. General Gordon was murdered by the Mad Mahdi in Khartoum. I read of it in *The Times*."

"That is what Mr Holmes called the rat up in our box room, My Lord, General Gordon."

The judge emitted a long, low growl of judicial displeasure.

"He killed it with the deadliest vegetable alkaloid known to man. It did not suffer." I took out my handkerchief and mopped my brow.

"Have I ever discussed the female sex with you, Doctor?"

"I say, Holmes —"

"You are still on oath, my friend. Would you describe me as a lady's man?"

I shook my head and then I frowned at a recollection. "I believe there was a lady that captured your attention."

There was a stir at the plaintiff's bench, and Miss Butterworth smiled demurely across the court at me.

"Could you describe her?"

"She was very beautiful, refined and highly intelligent. She had courage and she was extremely determined. I believe that you were captivated by those qualities more than by her looks. She eclipsed and predominated all other women, in your eyes."

Miss Butterworth blinked at me with a puzzled expression.

"Did you ever see this lady dressed as a man?" Holmes asked.

I reddened and smoothed my upper lip, *sans* moustache. "I believe that I did, outside our lodgings, but I cannot be sure."

A murmur of incredulity passed through the court.

The judge leaned across his desk, frowning. "A lady dressed as a man was outside your lodgings?"

"I believe she passed the time of day, no more," I answered.

"Passed the — who the devil was she?"

"I can say no more of that Your Honour, the good name of a lady is involved."

He banged his gavel. "Of course the good name of a lady is involved, Doctor, this is an action for breach of promise to wed!"

"I speak of another lady, not Miss Butterworth."

"Heavens help us, how many ladies are there in this case?"

Miss Butterworth swooned once again, and was helped from the court.

I craved the judge's permission to follow and minister to her. He nodded.

"A moment," said Holmes. "One last question and I am done with this witness, Your Honour."

The judged sniffed permission.

"Doctor Watson, do you think that a man who could deceive a fond, loving woman could be a man of principle?"

I stood erect and lifted up my chin. "I do not. For my own part, I would scorn the man who ever proved false to a woman; I would not trust him in any other matter."

Holmes nodded and I stepped down from the witness box, retrieved my medical bag from the bench where I had left it, and made for the door.

The judge stopped me. "Doctor, am I to understand that the defendant, Mr Sherlock Holmes is a friend of yours?"

"He is my closest friend, My Lord."

The judge looked from Holmes to me, and back again, shook his head and muttered under his breath.

I revived Miss Butterworth and helped her back into the chamber where she was received with supportive smiles and applause.

The prosecutor stood and said that his closing speech would be short. He clearly thought that his work was done.

"A gay deceiver is no enviable character for any respectable man to wear," he began. "No man of mental or moral worth would voluntarily assume it and go about his daily life with no tincture of remorse. Lord Byron tells us that

"Man's love is of man's life a thing apart —
Tis woman's whole existence.

This case is as cruel and a wicked a one as was ever put before a jury. This unhappy maiden has not only been treated with great brutality, she has been deceived as to the very name and character of her tormentor. With what a mean spirit did this *Holmes* or this *Escott* walk out with Miss Butterworth and plight his troth merely to increase his knowledge of bee-keeping? What a callous disregard for a maiden's feelings, and for her good name!"

A menacing growl came from the jury box and gallery as Sir Vandissart regarded his client with a sorrowful look. "Hers is in fact a double loss, for if Mr Holmes, or his wily alias Escott, had not offered marriage to her, then the under gardener at Appledore Towers would have. She might even now be in a state of married bliss with a stalwart ex-mariner, instead of in the thrall of the heartless beast that stands before you in the dock."

He inserted his monocle and peered across the courtroom at Holmes.

"Mr Holmes says that he is in favour of marriage — on the whole. He extolls the virtues of bigamy. This flippancy regarding the sacrament of marriage may be acceptable in the wilds of Utah, but we in Old England treat it with scorn and abhorrence."

There were loud shouts of approval from the gallery, and cries of 'hear, hear' from the jury box.

"Now, Mr Holmes may say that a spinster coming to a court of justice, and saying to him, 'You have taken my heart, give me your purse,' is in no very desirable position for a woman. To win the affections of an innocent young maiden like Miss Butterworth and then desert her is obviously a dastardly crime, but the defendant may argue that it is a crime of a character too ethereal to be touched by human law. If the woman's heart be shattered by the blow, what amount of compensation can heal the wound? Would not a woman of delicacy shrink from the publicity such cases generally confer on all the parties interested in them?

Maidens, like moths, are ever caught by glare,
And Mammon wins his way where seraphs might despair."

Miss Butterworth looked up at her counsel in bewilderment.

"There is no doubt," Sir Vandissart continued, his thumbs behind his lapels, " that women who bring breach of promise cases lower themselves and all their sex in our estimation. Perhaps the best advice one could give to those poor deceived shepherdesses is to try and forget their faithless swains and leave them to the stings and reflections of their own consciences, which will be a far greater punishment to them than parting with thousands (or even tens of thousands) of gold and silver."

Miss Butterworth glared at Sir Vandissart, and I hefted my medical bag in preparation for the inevitable swoon. The prosecutor turned and pointed an accusing finger at the defendant.

"However, gentlemen of the jury, the fiend that stands before you, this *Holmes-Escott* creature, this base deceiver, has not shown a particle of remorse. He has mocked the court with his mind-reading nonsense and caused poor Miss Butterworth to faint quite away. Think not then on compensation as you decide what damages this lovelorn damsel should receive as the victim of the monster's heartless wiles; condole with her distress and think of a heavy troy weight of atonement!"

Sir Vandissart resumed his seat to general applause.

Holmes stood, approached the jury benches, grasped his lapels and flexed his elbows.

"Love: I confess myself to be incredulous on the subject of love; I am immune to fervour, mad adoration and joy unbounded, and cynical perhaps in my view of the conventional moping, sighing and panting.

"I expect that you, members of the jury, would remind me that, with revenge, envy, blind hatred and sexual deviance, love is one of the most oft-cited and compelling motives for murder, and naturally, of suicide."

The jury gaped at Holmes in dark hostility, the judge's brows furrowed, the prosecutor smiled and the plaintiff, from her expression, hovered on the edge of hysteria.

Mr Pertwee shook his head. "Our client is committing self-murder."

Holmes chuckled to himself. "But that is all really by-the-by; I really do owe this young lady an apology. In all the excitement of the case that I was pursuing,

Though her beauty rare

172

Shame the blushing roses

I not only forgot that I had proposed to her, I forgot about her completely; she did not cross my mind at all. It was very remiss of me. I am the first to admit that I am rather absent-minded in such matters. And so, here we are."

He shrugged, smiled at the jury and resumed his seat.

The court erupted, and I truly feared that the jury might descend on Holmes and do him actual bodily harm.

The judge banged his gavel, the usher wielded his stave and order was restored. Miss Butterworth sat as though in a trance; she seemed not to have enough energy to swoon.

The judge glared down at the jury over his spectacles and made his summation. "The defendant held out to this personable young maiden a prize of matrimony to a rising young tradesman; a match to her advantage. That he used a false name and had no intention in fulfilling his engagement gives the poor, deceived girl a claim to heavy compensation."

The jurymen nodded to each other, looking pleased. The judge turned to Holmes. "And what a character the defendant now gives himself! A more melancholy exhibition I never have witnessed. By his own account he is on speaking terms with members of the criminal fraternity, has taken drugs and been engaged in various disgusting activities in his sitting room, including concocting deadly poisons." The judge's voice became hoarse with emotion. "He has referred to a dead rat by the appellation of one of our greatest military heroes." He nodded to the usher, and stood.

The usher banged his stave on the floor. "Pray be upstanding for one minute's silence in honour of General Gordon, hero of Khartoum!"

We stood, and in the silence I could almost hear the venom rising against Holmes. The usher banged his stave again and we sat.

"The question arises," the judge continued, facing the jury, "was the statement of Mr Holmes' many and varied faults characteristic of him, or was it assumed? Is he the worthless fellow he pretends to be, or is that character put on for the present decision? It is my view that, instead of playing the virtuous role (Oliver Cromwell as he so inaptly characterises himself), the defendant here makes himself out to be a ne'ere-do-well in the hopes that you, the jury, will think the plaintiff better off without him and forego the awarding of significant damages for the severed engagement. Do not be fooled, gentlemen. Any man who could lead this charming, virtuous maiden along the primrose path to matrimony as *Escott*, and then disappear, give up the worthy trade of plumber, and reappear as *Holmes*, a practitioner in the be-smudged and unwholesome profession of private sneak, does not deserve your consideration. Your sympathies must be with this virtuous maiden, twice fainting as she regards the iniquity of her faithless swain. Your duty is simply to determine what very heavy penalty may be appropriate for such infamous conduct."

Cheers resounded through the court.

Holmes stood, and the cheers were replaced by jibes and jeers.

The judge looked down at him with distaste. "Mr Holmes, I am instructing the jury. Kindly sit down."

"But, My Lord, I merely wished to say that I was deeply moved by Your Lordship's words, and I now conceive it my duty to instantly marry Miss Agatha Butterworth." He strode across the court the plaintiff's bench and knelt before her. "If she will have me."

The court erupted and Miss Butterworth assembled enough of her faculties to swoon once more.

Holmes stood, dusted off his knees and returned to his bench. He turned to me. "There, Watson, I have thrown in the towel and agreed to marry Aggie. I will wire for accommodation, book the train to Gretna Green, and reserve the blacksmith's services." He frowned. "I believe that there is a waiting period."

"Holmes, you cannot mean it!"

He adjusted his cravat. "Duty, Watson; we are slaves to Duty."

Mr Pertwee stood. "The judge has adjourned the court. I believe the other side will want to talk. Will you second me, Doctor?"

We met Holmes, Mycroft, Lestrade and Wiggins in the colonnade outside the court building.

Mr Pertwee held out his hand. "The plaintiff has withdrawn her suit against you, Mr Holmes — genius, sir, if I may make so bold. Have you thought of a career at the Bar?"

"Such histrionics," said Mycroft offering his brother a cigar. "I had a nightmarish vision of you and Aggie in a cottage in Eastbourne with a brood of tiny Sherlocks terrorising the county."

"Come, old man," I said wringing my friend's hand. "Let us have a restorative at the Coal Hole."

"I think my plan worked, on the whole," said Holmes as he lay back on a banquette in the pub. He turned to me. "I am sorry that I could not let you in on my plot, Watson, nor Mrs Hudson, Bessie and Billy. You are a stranger to prevarication, old man, and I wanted to have to worm out descriptions of my little foibles from you. You are a loyal friend; it was like pulling teeth. I realized when you threw that tantrum against me that you had smoked out my plan and were enthusiastically throwing coals on the fire, ha ha."

I avoided Mr Pertwee's eye and nodded. "Of course, Holmes."

Mr Pertwee and I found a private nook as Holmes re-enacted his part in the courtroom for Wiggins and Lestrade. I slipped my private chequebook from my pocket and made a cheque out to Miss Butterworth's solicitors. "A hundred pounds I think you said, Mr Pertwee; Aggie will have her trousseau and furniture from Maples and Co." And, I thought, Holmes and I would have to pull our belts in for a month or so.

"Miss Aggie said that she would prefer gold to a cheque."

"She may go to the devil," I responded affably. "She has her under-gardening, aquatic swain, and she has missed her chance of misery with Mr Sherlock Holmes."

I shook my head as I recalled my friend's eccentricities. "She should be paying me."

###

The Moving Finger Writes

On a December morning in a year just after the Great War, I sat at my desk in the bow window of the study above my consulting rooms and felt a familiar sentimental urge to open my old tin despatch box and leaf through my notes on the cases of my friend Sherlock Holmes. It was a familiar desire, and one that I succumbed to more and more as I settled into old age, but on that occasion I had a reason; I had thought to pay a visit to Holmes at his retreat near Eastbourne, and, since we had thoroughly explored (more than thoroughly explored in my view) every aspect of the keeping of honey bees — his hobby, I usually brought with me a bundle of notes on interesting cases from our past association. He in turn would delve into his box of memorabilia and, with memories temporarily refreshed, we fading warriors would spend a pleasant evening or two summoning shadows from our shared past.

I looked up at my study window as the sky darkened and sleet whipped against the panes. Not a day for excursions, I decided. I stood and helped myself to a cup of coffee and a biscuit from the plate of Abernethys that my housekeeper, Bessie, always laid out on a side table. I settled myself by the fire in my old chair from our Baker Street lodgings and looked idly through one of my notebooks. The title page showed that the volume was from 1891, and I leaned back and sipped my wine as I recalled that year. I was then in private practice, with a set of rooms in a street stuffed with other practitioners, none of us doing much business as the winter of '90 was but a bitter memory and we were enjoying a mild and pleasant spring.

I had not seen Holmes since the previous year; he kept our old rooms in Baker Street, but I knew from an occasional message from him that he was on the Continent, acting for the French government on an affair of great moment.

I recalled that I was at my desk in my consulting room, idly flicking through the latest issue of the *Strand Magazine* and thinking that it might be a suitable publication for accounts of some of Holmes' cases, when the door opened and my page boy showed in a man wearing a threadbare black jacket, just too-short trousers, elastic-sided boots and with a thin moustache of the smart, racy style favoured by clerks in newspaper offices and insurance companies.

I was astonished when the man threw his bowler onto the hat stand, bounded across the room and slumped into my patients' chair.

"Something is afoot," he cried in Holmes voice, peeling off his moustache. "I scent a felonious tincture in the air; and Josephus Ballater is stirring in his lair in Shadwell. His tentacles reach out across the city; something is coming on; something big, no, something huge. Have you a cigarette, I am out?"

"Holmes!" I exclaimed. "I thought you were in Narbonne."

"Until yesterday, I was. And I shall have to return in a day or two; three at the most. But I heard a whisper on the wind as I passed through Paris that stayed me in that city. Another murmur sent me to Amsterdam, and it is from there that I returned home to greet my good friend Watson with late Christmas and early Easter greetings — the cigarette, old chap?"

I scrabbled in one of the drawers of my desk and passed him a packet of *Wild Woodbine*.

"I spent last evening in the Kings Arms in Cable Street, Shadwell," Holmes said, tapping a cigarette from the pack. "It is as shady a nook as you'd like for cracksmen, cat burglars and, of course, Herr Ballater."

"I've not heard of the fellow."

"He is a highly reputable dealer in jewellery, and a high-class fence. It goes without saying that he is an expert on diamonds and other gems. Ballater has a network of associates throughout Europe and the Americas; a tiara stolen from a railway magnate's wife in New York will have its stones cut and reset and be the hands of his co-operators in Antwerp in a trice. Light?"

I passed him a box of matches and a kidney dish to act as an ashtray.

He lit the cigarette, took a long puff and coughed. "You are on one of your health cures again, Watson; this cigarette is so old and dry, it is almost desiccated."

I reddened. "I am cutting down, Holmes. There is evidence that smoking is not as healthy a habit as is generally supposed; true, smoking soothes the mind, exercises the lungs and relaxes the system, but overindulgence in the practice weakens one's nervous energy and impairs both the digesting force of the stomach and the secreting force of the liver." I avoided his eyes. "Or so certain authorities believe."

Holmes sniffed and looked around my consulting room with an eagle eye. "No smoking, fresh curtains and a vase of daffodils in the hall. Your page has been scrubbed, new-uniformed and hair-cutted. You are being taken in hand, my dear fellow. A female apparition lurks behind the hat stand in your hallway. A relatively recent spirit, I would suggest; she has got as far as your hallway and your cigarette case, but no farther."

I stood and tapped a cigarette from my packet. "Your vaunted deductive reasoning fails you, for once, Holmes. My housekeeper is beginning the Spring Clean; she started with the page. You will recall that she was trained by Mrs Hudson."

He smiled his jaguar smile. "Ha! You writhe in this young lady's grip. She must be very comely."

I lit my cigarette with a match, inhaled and spluttered. It was vile.

"To business," Holmes said in a serious tone. "You know that I am not entirely devoid of resources; my spies flit through the dark passageways and courts of the East End and pick up snippets of plans, traces of confederacy. A caper is being planned; it is a proper job, as the criminal classes call a serious crime, put on by a nob, Herr Ballater."

Holmes stubbed his cigarette in the kidney dish and I followed his example. He smiled a wry smile. "I have no proof as yet that my doppelgänger, the evil genius whose movements I dog, is looking over Herr Ballater's shoulder; there are no paw prints, no direct links, but he is a will o' the wisp, a phantasm of evil." Holmes rubbed his hands together. "It will be no easy task to mark him down, but it is my solemn duty."

Holmes glanced at the magazine on my desk. "You seem very comfortable here, Watson; you do not appear to be overburdened with work."

I chuckled. "You should have seen the waiting room in December, Holmes. In this mild weather people have better things to do than to get sick."

"In that case, you wouldn't object if I asked you to join me in my enterprise against Herr Ballater?"

"I should be delighted. I have a young fellow next door, just starting out in general practice and very keen, who would be happy to take up the slack, and —"

The door of the consulting room slowly opened and my page poked his head in. "Miss Witherspoon," he whispered, rolling his eyes.

I blanched and stood. "I hope you won't think me too unconventional if I suggest that we leave by the side entrance, Holmes? Miss Witherspoon is, as you suggest, comely, but she is the daughter of a Baptist minister and of a commanding disposition; she can be difficult if her very decided views on a range of topics are ignored." I opened the desk drawer, slid the cigarette packet and kidney tray inside and smoothed my moustache. "She is also perhaps a trifle overly familiar."

The page winked and disappeared. Holmes stood, gave me a wry look, but said nothing. We picked up our hats, and I my medical bag, and I led Holmes to the side door and along a narrow alley to a gate that gave out into the street behind my own. A providential cab appeared and we were very soon alighting outside the facade of 221B Baker Street.

"It is good to be on English soil again," said Holmes, looking up to the windows of our sitting room.

Mrs Hudson welcomed us and we settled ourselves upstairs amid the familiar, homely clutter. The only odd aspect of the room was that, due to Holmes' prolonged absence, it did not stink of chemicals from his experiments.

"Here is my plan," said Holmes. "And may I say it is a great pleasure for me to be playing doubles with you again. If you prefer a less Witherspooned regime, you might like to take up residence again in your old rooms here; they are kept ready."

I instantly agreed.

"Very well, I have made a list of items for immediate action in the Ballater case —"

The doorbell rang, and in a moment Billy appeared at the door of the sitting room with a slip of paper on his salver. "For the Doctor. Mr Peterson's waiting downstairs for an answer having a nice cuppa tea with Mrs H."

I took the slip and read it. "It is a note by public messenger redirected from my house —" I looked up. "We must have just missed him as we made our escape. The message is from Doctor James Reid. I do not know him personally, but he mentions a mutual friend, Doctor Montague. You remember Montague,

Holmes; we visited him and his father at Dunsinon Abbey in Scotland."

"Vaguely. Ah, here is luncheon."

Mrs Hudson laid the table as I continued. "He asked permission to wait on me at two this afternoon. He also asks whether I am in contact with you."

"Oh, really, Watson, this is too inconsiderate; we are about to embark on a case, a proper job; possibly thousands of pounds worth of jewels may be at risk —"

I gave him an admonishing look. "Doctor Reid is Physician-in-Ordinary to Her Majesty the Queen, Holmes."

He subsided. "Oh, very well."

After luncheon, Holmes curled up in his chair in front of our crackling fire smoking his churchwarden pipe. I saw from the packet on the mantel that he had brought back with him some Dutch tobacco, and I filled one of my old pipes and joined him.

"I have tails on two suspects, Watson, both seen talking in a conspiratorial fashion to Herr Ballater, and neither known to me or to the Irregulars." He waved his notes. "I have exact descriptions of the fellows, but no clear picture of their intended target except for a few words overheard in a crowded noisy pub: 'diamonds, tiaras, pearls'; that's all"

"A jewellery shop?" I suggested.

"Or a house party at some ducal mansion."

The doorbell rang, and a few moments later, Billy ushered a middle-aged, tall, rather stooped gentleman into our sitting room. He had a narrow face, a receding hairline and he wore gold *pince-nez*. We made our introductions, and I offered Doctor Reid a place on our sofa. He declined all refreshment but gave Holmes and I ready permission to continue with our pipes.

"I saw Doctor Montague last month," he said in a strong voice with a Lowland Scots lilt. "He suggested that I lay a strange case before you, Mr Holmes. It is a matter of extreme sensitivity, and I must ask you and Doctor Watson for your word that whatever passes between us on the subject to which it is my heavy duty to allude, it be kept within these four walls."

I promised and Holmes waved acquiescence. "But really, Doctor Reid," he said with a smile, "more confessions have been heard in this room that at the Vatican."

I squirmed inwardly at Holmes' levity, but his quip found its mark with Doctor Reid, who laughed aloud. I recalled that he was a Scot, and probably Church of Scotland, or even Presbyterian, and likely no friend to Rome.

"I think that we might, without presuming on you to elaborate on the matter, come to certain conclusions," Holmes continued, puffing on his pipe. "You are physician to the Queen. You travel with her when she makes her trips from Windsor to Osborne on the Isle of Wight, Balmoral in Scotland and her annual excursion abroad. That much is public knowledge."

He leaned back in his chair. "It is known to a more exclusive circle that you are, now that the Prince Consort and John Brown, the Queen's ghillie, are deceased, possibly her closest confidant. I therefore conclude that your sensitive matter concerns the Queen."

Doctor Reid shifted uncomfortably in his chair. "A strange phenomenon has manifested itself at the castle, in the late Prince Consort's bedroom, in fact."

He sighed a long, weary sigh. "You are aware of the great distress Prince Albert's death caused Her Majesty; she was, to a significant degree, deranged with grief and she had the status and means to ensure that the expression of her grief, however overwrought, was made manifest."

Holmes and I frowned as we tried to decipher Doctor Reid's meaning. He looked up. "I am sorry, gentlemen, I am somewhat overwrought myself and I am not making much sense. I am suffering from lack of sleep, overwork and, above all, *Munshimania*." He laughed a shrill laugh and again writhed in his chair.

I turned to Holmes and frowned; he instantly stood and looked at his watch. "Doctor Reid, I must apologise. I have forgotten a most pressing engagement. Might I leave you with Doctor Watson for —"

Holmes glanced at me and I surreptitiously showed two fingers.

"An hour or two? We might then take tea together."

Doctor Reid smiled and gave his assent. Holmes fetched his hat and coat from his room and left us alone.

"Colleague," I said in a firm tone. "I have my medical bag with me. Let us have a look at that boil on your neck, and what I believe may be another on your leg."

Doctor Reid demurred, but he had not the energy to argue with me and he was persuaded. I lanced a painful boil, and treated a carbuncle on his thigh with a warm compress. I took the doctor's temperature and found him slightly febrile, so I placed a cool flannel on his brow and asked Mrs Hudson to send to the Italian coffee shop down the road for a pot of cold minestrone soup.

"Now, Doctor," I said when Doctor Reid was comfortable on our sofa, covered with a light cotton sheet. "We both know that fevers, boils and other skin problems are commonly associated with overwork, sleeplessness and emotional stress. But you mentioned another possible cause."

He chuckled. "*Munshimania*."

Holmes returned to find that Doctor Reid had left.

"Doctor Reid insisted that he must return to Windsor or the Queen would be discommoded," I said. "He is not a well man."

Holmes settled in his chair by the fire. "I called on my brother Mycroft at the War Office while you ministered to your colleague. He was willing to talk of Doctor Reid, but not of the matter that the doctor wishes us to investigate. He suggested that it is a state secret and I could not move him. And yet he chuckled as I left. It is annoying. Is the tea fresh?"

I went to the door and called downstairs for Billy.

"I did glean some information," Holmes continued. "Her Majesty enjoys rude good health for her age, but is insomniac, calling for the duty maids several times each night and sending them to early graves. I understand that Doctor Reid is obliged to wait on Her Majesty five or many more times a day even though he does not examine her (she has a morbid fear of stethoscopes). His duties are not confined to medical matters. Doctor Reid acts as a go-between when schisms and crises arise in the Court: such troubles flourish in the close atmosphere of purposeless communities — monasteries, courts and parliaments."

"I say, Holmes —"

"His stooped appearance, the worry lines on his face, his pale complexion (forgive me for treading on your medical toes, Watson), his general air of strain and fatigue suggest that he is over-worked and overburdened."

Holmes stood, refilled his pipe from the packet on the mantel and lit it from the fire with a spill.

"Naturally, the trials and tribulations at Windsor focus around Her Majesty. Her concerns are thus: keeping the memory of her late husband, the Prince Consort, alive; rehabilitating the memory of her previous confidant, John Brown (who was cordially loathed by the members of the Household), and protecting her Indian servants, generally considered a pernicious influence on Her Majesty, from what

185

she considers snobbish and racial abuse. Have I touched on the matter of Doctor Reid's concern?"

"To a degree: the affair certainly involves Prince Albert, John Brown and the Indians, but it is a question of ghosts."

Holmes groaned and slumped into his chair. "I had thought were rid of them. Is the ghillie ghost howling through Windsor Castle screeching drunken imprecations in Gaelic? Is the Prince Consort walking through walls and are the Indian servants conjuring evil spirits in the mangle room?"

"We will take luncheon with Doctor Reid and Mr Henry Ponsonby at Windsor tomorrow, Holmes," I said firmly. "And we can see for ourselves."

"But what of Herr Ballater?"

I raised my eyebrows. "He must wait his turn, Holmes. We act for the Queen."

Holmes threw up his hands in mock despair.

"I prescribed a month of complete rest for Doctor Reid," I continued, ignoring my friend's histrionics. "I do not think he will get it. The Queen obviously leans on him in her grief, which according to Doctor Reid is her natural state, as she did John Brown."

Holmes muttered something illiberal under his breath.

"The Queen's Indian servants cause a fuss; especially Abdul Karim, her so-called Indian secretary or *munshi*." I tapped out my pipe on the grate. "Indians require a firm hand, as I learned in Afghanistan. Treated well and without undue familiarity, they make excellent servants. They are as clean as cats, look charming in their uniforms and are very biddable."

Holmes looked despairingly at the list of measures we had compiled. "I must deploy the Irregulars."

I went home, keeping a keen eye out for Miss Witherspoon, packed an overnight bag, left a message for my fellow practitioner next door and returned to Baker Street where Holmes and I spent a very pleasant evening catching up on our news and planning our campaign against Herr Ballater.

The following morning, Holmes and I took a fast train from Paddington and arrived in Windsor. We were met at the station by Doctor Reid and conveyed by carriage into the castle grounds and to the office of Sir Henry Ponsonby, Private Secretary to the Sovereign, on the ground floor of the Augusta Tower. He was a tall gentleman with a neat beard who behaved with courtly courtesy but had a twinkle of humour in his eyes.

"It is very good of you to come at such short notice, gentlemen," Sir Henry said after we had made our introductions. He looked down at his toes — I followed his gaze and noticed that he, like Holmes' clerk impersonation, wore elastic-sided boots. "I am sure that Doctor Reid conveyed to you the absolute need for secrecy in this most distressing matter, but I do not know if he clarified our position — mine and his — with regard to Her Majesty and especially the Prince of Wales. Neither must have an *inkling* that we have introduced a private detective into the Castle. That is an absolute necessity."

Holmes stood and picked up his hat. "Consulting detective, in fact, Sir Henry. Doctor Watson and I have no wish to intrude. We will wish you a very good day."

Sir Henry sighed. "There, I have offended you, sir. I unreservedly apologise. But I am sure that you will, on reflection, understand that my often painful duty is to transmit the wishes, opinions and commands of Her Majesty to those of her subjects with whom she desires to communicate. I am, as it were, on the front line. It is an invidious position to occupy, and one that causes me a good deal of soul-searching. However, facts are facts, and I must not gloss them: Her Majesty would be stricken and the Prince of Wales would be livid, if your

187

presence here were made known to them. It is wearisome, but it is a constraint we must be aware of."

He smiled a brilliant smile. "And the occurrence is rather curious, Mr Holmes; a very odd thing. Reid and I are utterly perplexed."

Holmes returned Sir Henry's smile. "Then I shall not make your work more arduous by playing the *pezzonovante*."

I looked blankly at him.

"A male primadonna."

I coughed to suppress a snigger as Holmes turned back to Sir Henry. "May we see the phenomenon?"

Sir Henry stood, opened an inner door and nodded to a tall, handsome young man in livery with a knowing look about him who waited outside. The footman ran up a set of stairs and disappeared around a corner. "Archer will reconnoitre ahead, but we should be safe enough. The Prince is about his occasions elsewhere in the kingdom, and the Queen is much taken up with preparations for our theatrical entertainment this evening. Mr D'Oyly Carte presents *The Gondoliers*, a confection by Sir Arthur Sullivan. The rooms of the Queen and the Ladies of the Household are a flurry of silk and lace as they engage in their *couture*."

The footman appeared around the corner and gestured that the way was clear. We followed him along several rather over-decorated corridors to an ornate door outside which a small portrait of Prince Albert stood on a side table, surrounded by flowers.

"This is the Blue Room, the Prince-Consort's suite," Sir Henry explained. "Herr Löhlein was valet to Prince Albert until his death in 1861. He remained with the Household (most of the Prince's staff were assimilated into the Queen's — not without friction) until he died in 1886." He indicated the footman. "Archer then took over Herr Löhlein's duties."

I frowned and gave the footman a puzzled look. "But why would the deceased prince need a valet?"

"Perhaps I could show you, gentlemen," said Archer with a grin. He opened the heavy door and letting out a very strong scent of flowers. We preceded him into a large bedroom decorated in lush blue and gold. A huge garlanded bust of the Prince Consort stood on a plinth between two beds dominating the room. A desk, dressing table, sofa and washstand were the other principal furnishings. Heavy silk curtains, open and tied with gold-tasselled rope, matched the blue silk wall hangings. Bouquets of spring flowers and fronds of cypress lay on the beds.

"As you can see, gentlemen," said Archer, "nothing has been touched since the Prince Consort passed. The handkerchief that he last used lies on the sofa and his hat and gloves are laid out ready for his afternoon stroll. Should he decide to write a note or letter, the blotting book on his desk is open with a pen and ink upon it. I wind his watch every night and place it on its night stand. Her Majesty casts fresh white flowers and cypress over his bed every morning."

"The room is kept exactly as it was when the prince was alive," Holmes said. "That is most remarkable."

"There are more flowers than he would have liked, but essentially, yes."

Sir Henry sighed. "The Prince's daily routine is strictly adhered to."

Archer nodded. "Every morning I strop Prince Albert's razor, raise a lather on his shaving stick and spread tooth powder on his brush. I lay out the prince's clothes — either clothes suitable for the engagements of the day, or several suits of clothes for him to choose from. Later in the morning, I supervise as the sheets are changed and fresh towels replace the used ones."

Archer smoothed a ruck on the bed cover. "In the afternoon, I lay out his evening clothes and bring fresh water —"

A knock came at the door and Archer opened it and collected a bowl and a jug of hot water from a maid. With the air of a stage conjurer, he placed the bowl on Prince Albert's dressing table and filled it with hot water. Steam rose from the bowl and condensation covered the mirror. Three lines of writing immediately appeared.

"German," said Archer. "It's from HRH."

"Yes, it's from Prince Albert," said Sir Henry peering at the mirror. "Brown was barely literate in English; his messages are rarely legible."

Holmes examined the writing through his magnifying glass. "Strong capitals, thick print; written with a pudgy finger with nails pared to the quick. It seems that the writer is concerned about British interests in Matabeleland; he urges the government to adhere to the terms of our ultimatum to Portugal of last year and use active measures to clear out all Portuguese troops, and particularly missionaries, from the region. He also suggests that, in India, Hindu feasts should be scheduled so that they do not clash with Muslim ones, and that the grant of land accorded to the *Munshi* in his native Agra is really rather meagre, considering his loyal service."

I frowned.

"Matabeleland is near our Cape Colony in Africa, I believe," Holmes explained. He turned to Sir Henry. "The *Munshi* is Her Majesty's Indian Secretary — a Muslim?"

"Indeed. The painful issue of riots during the Muslim procession of *Muharam* is alluded to. The more common messages from His Royal Highness are warnings not to trust Russia and comments on Bimetallic Question." He sniffed. "The handwriting has been attested by Her Majesty as authentically Prince Albert's."

Holmes turned to Archer. "You place a bowl of hot water on Prince Albert's dressing table under the mirror every morning?"

"I do."

"Is the mirror wiped each day?"

"Not since the messages started, but the window is opened two inches from three to four in the afternoon to circulate the air."

"Even now?" I asked.

He nodded. "The routine remains the same as when HRH lived."

"That clears the mirror, of course," said Holmes. "It is ready for the next message. Are there any manifestations in the afternoon? Any ghostly writing?"

"None," Archer replied.

Sir Henry thanked the footman and dismissed him. "Ah, gentlemen," said Archer from the door. "You won't move anything, will you? Her Majesty comes each night to say a prayer and she gets in a tizz if anything is out of place."

Sir Henry nodded curtly and waved him away.

"You see what I am up against?" he asked as the door closed. "You heard what the fellow said of the Queen-Empress? 'She gets in a tizz.'" He sat on the edge of the bed and pulled out a large white handkerchief from his pocket. "And, between ourselves, gentlemen, she does, especially now with the *Munshi* on four-month's leave in India."

He mopped his brow. "The messages have caused great unrest in the household. They are a curious mix of foreign policy edicts, diktats on financial matters and advice on domestic issues: on the treatment of the servants mostly. The writer thinks that Her Majesty's Indian servants, particularly the *Munshi*, are poorly treated by the Household."

He frowned. "That is in fact rather odd. The Indian servants were acquired well after the death of the Prince Consort; I wonder that he has an opinion on them. And John Brown loathed them with a drunken Scottish passion."

"Perhaps the political notes are a blind," I suggested. "A disaffected servant may be trying to gain favour with Her Majesty."

"Archer," Holmes suggested.

"Sir Henry shook his head and smiled a half-smile. "Perhaps. What makes all this even more ludicrous is that, if these are indeed communications from Prince Albert, then the notes are privileged and secret: the Queen insists as much. I therefore have the sorry duty to convey the content of the communications, at least those from the Prince, to the Prime Minister via confidential messenger."

"And what is Lord Salisbury's view of the matter?"

"He has not deigned to offer one; he has remained silent on the subject. The Queen is uncomfortable with the Prime Minister's silence and she urges me to brace him and secure a promise that her late husband's wishes, particularly on financial and foreign policy matters, will be adhered to."

"Are the view's expressed in today's messages typical of the prince?" Holmes asked.

Sir Henry considered. "Politically, he is of the opinion that we must take a firmer line with Lisbon and Saint Petersburg, and offer greater support to the Porte and Moslems generally."

He mopped his brow again. "Financially — well, actually the fiscal advice is quite sound, according to the Treasury. Prince Albert was surprisingly adept at figures, for a German nobleman. He never quite figured out our pounds, shillings and pence, but he could manage guineas well enough."

I am ashamed to say that I had to suppress a giggle and Sir Henry frowned at me.

"And John Brown?" asked Holmes.

"When he is legible, he too counsels fiscal thrift —"

Holmes nodded. "A Scottish virtue."

"And the strong thread through the domestic messages is that we should treat the *Munshi* with more respect, and to stop gossiping about the fellow."

"I gather that Doctor Reid has no high opinion of the Her Majesty's Indian Secretary," I said.

Sir Henry laughed. "Poor Reid gets the brunt of the Queen's complaints at his treatment by the Household. Ha! She knows that she would get short shift from me."

He considered. "Now that Abdul Karim has been raised (at Her Majesty's vehement insistence) from footman to his present illustrious rank of *Munshi*, he is perfectly ludicrous with his airs and graces and claims of precedence. Yes, the fellow is tiresome, but he is not all bad; he keeps the other Indians in line — without him there would be even more fuss and bother. Look at the Highlanders now that Brown is gone! No, I do not share the opinion of the Gentlemen of the Household that the *Munshi* is a pernicious influence. We have been run ragged by Her Majesty while he is away; I look forward to his return, which should be sometime soon."

Sir Henry sighed again. "He will give the Queen something to do."

He stood and adjusted his cravat in the mirror. "But advice from a deceased royal prince and a dead ghillie — you see our quandary, gentlemen, and I very much hope that you can help us find a solution to this mystery. Have you seen enough?"

He opened the door and started as he saw Archer leaning against the opposite wall of the corridor. The footman held up a key. "Got to lock up after."

"Who has a key to this room, other than you?" Holmes asked him.

"The Steward of the castle and me, sir: just the two."

"Not the Queen?"

"I open the door for Her Majesty in the morning, and again at ten in the evening when she likes to say a little prayer and bid the prince goodnight."

Sir Henry turned to Holmes and I. "Doctor Reid has invited you gentlemen for luncheon. I will not join you, as I have to oversee the arrangements for our operetta. I understand that there are no less than eighty performers for whom we must provide facilities. And Empress Frederick of Germany is currently visiting her mother with her retinue, which will stretch our resources still further."

"Has anyone stood vigil in the Prince's room overnight?" Holmes asked. "It is the obvious move."

Sir Henry paled. "They have not. If the Queen —" He glanced at Archer.

"I understand," said Holmes.

Sir Henry directed Archer to show us to the Norman Gate, where Doctor Reid and his wife lived. He and Holmes engaged in soft conversation as we passed along corridors and up and down stairs and I gawped at the amazing collection of paintings that adorned the walls, and at the huge variety of bric-a-brac set on tables lining the corridors.

Doctor Reid and his wife were most welcoming. They occupied a very pleasant suite of rooms with a charming view of Eton School across the river. We sat down to a luncheon of salmon with boiled potatoes, washed down with chilled Hock.

"Irish salmon, I'm afraid, gentlemen," said Doctor Reid. "We will have to wait a few weeks for the true Scottish."

"Oh, James," cried his wife. "The fishmonger guaranteed the salmon was fresh from the River Drowes. I presumed it was in Scotland."

"Ireland, my dear."

Madame Reid pouted, bent her head and attended to her plate.

"You catch us at something of a bad time," her husband continued. "March is a dark time for the Household, although the Queen is usually in good spirits. She does love a nice funeral or a service of remembrance, and we have not only Prince Albert this month, we also have the Queen's mother, Princess Victoria. Her Majesty is never more exalted than when she is wallowing in grief. It is a trying period for the Ladies and Gentlemen of the Household, however."

He refilled our glasses. "Actually, I should say that such remembrance services take place very regularly throughout the year. We mark the anniversaries of as many deaths as Her Majesty desires, including those of dogs and even housemaids."

After luncheon, Doctor Reid suggested that we accompany him up to the battlements to enjoy the splendid view.

"Perhaps the doctor would prefer a cup of tea," suggested Mrs Reid with a pitiful glance at me.

Much to my colleague's and Holmes' surprise, I accepted tea and they left for the battlements without me.

Mrs Reid glanced at the closed door, crossed the room and sat beside me on the sofa. "I would like to thank you, Doctor, for your treatment of my poor husband's honourable wounds. I have been nagging him for weeks to see a doctor, but you know what doctors are — he was as stubborn as a —" She patted my arm. "Oh, dear, Doctor Watson, I meant no affront!"

I smiled. "No offence taken, M'am. You are perfectly correct: we physicians are a stubborn breed."

Madam Reid took my hand. "You have no idea what my poor helpmate has to endure: the servants! I could tell you tales — but hush." She put her fan to her lips and blinked soulfully at me. "But I do them no injustice if I say that they are surly, under-employed and overly familiar fellows — even some of the maids. And the Highlanders! They are in a constant state of extra-ordinary drunkenness." She dropped her voice to a whisper. "The Indian servants are also in a constant state over some imagined slight, or an affront to their *amour propre*. They can do no wrong in the Queen's eyes; Her Majesty expects the Gentlemen of the Household to *dine* with the *Munshi*! Think of it! Not so long ago he was a footman, and now he is Indian Secretary to the Queen despite an inability to write properly in either his language or ours. And the smells! Curry at all hours, and the men perfume themselves like, like — it really is intolerable. The Ladies and Gentlemen of the Household are in a state of turmoil. It is too, too utterly —"

Happily for me, Doctor Reid and Holmes entered the room and joined us by the fire.

Mrs Reid blinked back tears. "I was just saying, Mr Holmes, how kind it was of Doctor Watson to minister to my dear, dear husband yesterday. I am so very, very grateful."

Reid and I avoided each other's eyes.

"You will excuse me, gentlemen," said Mrs Reid with a frown that suggested she had noticed our discomfort. "I have an appointment with my seamstress. One must look one's best at the opera this evening."

Mrs Reid left us, and I sighed an inward sigh of relief. "I was astonished by the extra-ordinary number of fine paintings that adorn the castle walls," I said to start a conversational hare.

"I saw a Fra Angelico, and some other interesting Italian and German primitives outside the Prince-Consort's room," said Holmes with a smile. "I immediately thought how easy it would be to cut the paintings out of their frames, roll them up, put them under my arm and stroll out the main gate of the castle."

Doctor Reid looked at him in astonishment.

I chuckled. "You mustn't mind Holmes. Crime is his *metier*."

"We don't experience a great deal of crime," said Doctor Reid as he smiled an uncertain smile. "I suppose the Guards on patrol with fixed bayonets keep the criminal classes at bay."

"No crime?" asked Holmes in what I thought was a tone of mild disappointment.

Doctor Reid considered. "No serious crime. Most servants have been with the Royal Household for many years, and some families have worked here for generations. Petty crimes are never checked, of course."

"What sort of crimes?" he asked.

"Drunkenness mostly, and thus insubordination and breakages. The Highlanders serve at dinner and far more soup is slopped over one than goes into the bowl; the crash of falling plates is a constant cacophony. Let me think. One of Her Majesty's brooches was supposedly lost, and her Dresser was disciplined. In fact, it was pawned in town by one of the Indian servants. The *Munshi* persuaded the Queen that wretch had found it and that it was the custom in his country for finders to be keepers; Her Majesty ordered the Gentlemen of the Household not to discuss the matter any further, and no action was taken."

He opened a fine humidor and we took cigars.

"We had a pair of footmen thieving silver cutlery; they were caught red-handed, but even then Sir Henry had the devil of a job getting them discharged."

He blew a stream of cigar smoke towards the windows. "A pair of brothers from a village in darkest mid-Wales."

For some unaccountable reason, Holmes looked across at me and winked!

Doctor Reid coughed and looked rather abashed. "Now, I have arranged a pleasant suite of rooms for you. And — ahem — for you to have dinner in your suite." He glanced up as if to gauge our reactions. "Sir Henry and I will dine with the Queen and we will be forced into knee breeches and stockings; it is wearisome in the extreme."

Holmes smiled. "I gather that doctors and detectives are not well thought of at Court; we are kept below the salt, if we are invited at all."

Doctor Reid returned Holmes' smile. "When I came to Windsor, about ten years ago, I was not invited to join the Gentlemen of the Household at dinner, but I was allowed to breakfast with them as that meal is buffet-style and the Gentlemen could hide from common interlopers behind their copies of *The Times*. I was permitted to join them for an occasional lunch. That suited me very well, in fact."

He sighed. "But now I have to dine. In sober truth, gentlemen, meals are perfectly sepulchral. There are so few topics bland enough for us to discuss, and on those we are already fully aware of everyone's views. If we stray into controversy, the Queen calls out the name of one of her dogs, and has a long loud chat with it. The only bright element, from the Household point of view, is that the Queen eats voraciously, but speedily; seldom does any meal last more than thirty minutes."

He laughed. "You must think our existence here is perfectly fatuous, gentlemen; at times I do myself. If I were without the comfort of a happy home and several fine colleagues, like Sir Henry, I could not stand it. The occasional entertainment, as tonight, also helps. We have had tableaux before, but *The Gondoliers* will be the first professional theatrical entertainment at Court since The Passing."

Madame Reid put her head around the door and waved a flimsy. "A telegram has arrived for you, Mr Holmes," she said in a wondering voice.

"Thank you. I took the liberty of giving your address to one of my colleagues in case of emergency. I hope I did not discommode you."

"Not at all," she said in a tone that strongly suggested otherwise.

Holmes put the telegram in his pocket unread. "I may need to reply. Is there a telegraph office in the Castle?" He made a note of Doctor Reid's directions on his cuff, and stood. "Thank you for a most informative conversation, Doctor and Madame."

"And a fine luncheon," I added.

"Watson and I might take an invigorating walk through the grounds, if that is permissible?"

"You might stop at Sir Henry's office," Doctor Reid suggested. "He can give you the key to your rooms and a guide."

We found our way downstairs and stepped out of an archway and into the Castle Yard.

"A state of war clearly exists between the Highlanders, the Indian servants and the Household," Holmes suggested as we followed Doctor Reid's directions to the telegraph office. "The Queen has always championed underdogs, thus her partiality for Turkey rather than Russia."

"The Russians are guilty of numerous atrocities, Holmes."

"There were atrocities on both sides."

"Ha!" I answered. We continued our stroll for a while in companionable silence.

"And what of the Prince's bedroom?" Holmes asked as we neared the telegraph office.

I considered. "Her Majesty obviously goes there to, ah, how shall I put it — commune with her husband's spirit."

"Commune suggests that there are two parties involved," said Holmes with a grin. "You accept the notion of an apparition, or rather, an unlikely pair of spectres, Prince Albert and John Brown?"

"Hardly. The Queen obviously indulges in nostalgic —"

"Tut tut, Doctor," said Holmes wagging a finger at me. "Queen-Empresses do not indulge."

I spluttered an incoherent reply as Holmes slipped the telegram out of his pocket, opened it and read it.

He nodded to himself and disappeared into the telegraph office. I took the opportunity to buy a couple of packets of cigarettes from a passing vendor before we made our way to Sir Henry's office to pick up our bags and the key to our lodgings. We entered the office and were immediately assailed by a delicious aroma.

"Coffee?" Sir Henry offered. "I have a supply of the true Orinoco bean from a pal in the War Office. The Navy is mapping the Venezuelan coast in case the fellows get fractious again, and we occasionally send a gunboat upriver to reconnoitre (the First Lord is partial to fresh Orinoco coffee)."

We gladly accepted and he passed us tiny cups of excellent coffee.

"I had your luggage sent to your rooms," he said. "And a page is on hand to escort you."

"Very well," said Holmes. "I should like to request a couple of items that will aid us in our investigation —"

Sir Henry smiled and passed Holmes a sealed packet. "This is the Steward's key to the Blue Room; I thought you might want it. He asked me to remind you gentlemen that there is no question of your spending any part of the night in the Prince Consort's rooms, even on the sofa. I must ask for your assurances on the matter."

"You have them," said Holmes airily. "Neither of us shall enter the room until morning."

Sir Henry gave Holmes a puzzled look, but said nothing.

"Might we also crave your indulgence and request a pair of revolvers and ammunition," Holmes continued.

Sir Henry laughed. "I wonder what class of apparition you are expecting, Mr Holmes, but I can easily accede to your request. You have come to the right shop for weapons: Windsor Castle is an armoury. I could let you have a suit of armour, a blunderbuss or a twelve-pounder cannon, if you have need. You might also care for a squad of Scots Guards, we have plenty."

Holmes considered. "Just the pistols, for now, thank you. I might have employment for the guards later this evening. The opera starts at what time?"

"At nine, in the Waterloo Chamber."

Holmes stood.

"Thank you for the coffee," I said, standing with him.

"By the way," said Holmes. "What were the names of the two footmen you discharged recently for theft?"

"Evans, Peter and, let me see, Evans, Gareth; brothers."

"Of Welsh extraction?"

"I believe so, they had slight accents."

We thanked Sir Henry and followed a page up yet more stairs and along yet more corridors.

"We will not wait in the Prince's room for the apparition to appear?" I asked.

"No, no. I think we may get an uninterrupted night's sleep. There is no need for vigils."

"And the pistols?"

"Our quarry may very well be armed. We must be prepared."

That evening, we watched as lines of chairs were assembled in front of an improvised stage in the Waterloo Chamber. A large armchair for Her Majesty and a line of gilt chairs for her distinguished guests were screened from the rest of the audience by potted plants.

A short young man in with ginger hair in a loud check suit appeared before us.

"Wiggins!" I exclaimed. "How did you get into the Castle?"

"I joined the cast and crew from the Savoy as they unloaded scenery and such from the train. I just picked up a box of props and sauntered in with the others. The Savoy mob thought I was with the Castle, and vice versa."

He laughed. "It was a right palaver, getting all the stuff off the train. I could have dipped a dozen watches and pocketbooks, but I just took the one wipe, to keep in practice, like." He held up a fine silk handkerchief.

I frowned. "What infernal —"

Holmes laughed. "Look, there is a monogram: 'R D'O C', Richard D'Oyly Carte, the producer of the Sullivan plays."

"A frightful business, Holmes."

"Ah, here is Archer," said Holmes as the footman saw us and walked across the room.

"Am I right in thinking that almost all of the Castle staff will be involved in the arrangements for the theatricals?" Holmes asked him.

"Indeed sir, we are busy with the theatre here in the Waterloo Chamber, and with refreshments for the Reception afterwards. And those servants that are free will try to sneak in at the back of the room to see *The Gondoliers*. It's the first Royal Performance since you-know-who passed on."

I frowned at the man's impertinence. It looked as though Mrs Reid's comments on the unruliness of the Windsor staff were true.

"It'll be all a-glitter, Mr Holmes," Archer continued. "A fine sight. And the real thing, too — diamonds; no paste for the Queen and Empress Frederick."

I smiled as I saw Holmes' eyes sparkle.

Archer pursed his lips. "Mind you, the Queen may just wear her black clothes and white bonnet like usual; you never know. If the throng is all twinkling with diamonds, Her Majesty goes plain; she likes plain and she likes to stand out by going simple. Like in *The Gondoliers*." He grinned and sang in a pleasant tenor.

> *"When you have nothing else to wear*
> *But cloth of gold and satins rare*
> *For cloth of gold you cease to care —*
> *Up goes the price of shoddy."*

He smiled. "I'm in the Household choir."

Holmes frowned. "Do your duties bring you into contact with Abdul Karim, the Queen's Indian Secretary?"

"The *Munshi*? He's all over everything, he is. Suits us footmen, though; used to be us standing about for hours in the Park while HM had breakfast or went through her boxes from the Prime Minister. Now it's the Indians. And it's no fun even inside — HM insists that no room should be heated above sixty degrees; there are thermometers by every fireplace and she checks them regular. And then there's the afternoon ride, with all the Ladies and Gents of the Household trotting along beside her donkey cart puffing and blowing: ha! No, I've nothing against the *Munshi*, he earns his pay."

"Does he mix with the other servants?"

"Not a lot, the Indians keep to themselves in the King John Tower mostly; gawd the curry smells! But they're friendly enough, if they pick up the lingo. The *Munshi's* not above having a chat or lending ten bob to a bloke that's short. He puffs up now and then, but we're used to that with the nobs."

He lowered his voice. "There was talk of the whole Household — everyone downstairs, I mean — having Urdu lessons like the Queen gets from the *Munshi*; she wanted to order us in Indian, not English, see. The Highlanders got narked (they don't even like speaking English, let alone foreign) and Sir Henry put his foot down."

Archer grinned. "He's a talker, is the *Munshi*; he's got a good line of blather, like an Irishman. He talks about India with HM, and she goes all soft; Her Majesty is very taken with all things Indian."

"Here is Sir Henry, Holmes," I said stiffly as Archer stepped back a respectful distance. I saw that I was still holding Mr Carte's handkerchief and I hastily put it behind my back as Sir Henry took out his own handkerchief and mopped his brow. "Well, well, we are progressing, although it doesn't look like it. I heard the orchestra rehearsing the overture; I must say Mr Sullivan has produced some charming, lively melodies. Have you, ah, gentlemen —" Sir Henry faltered a little as he looked Wiggins up and down. "Have you seen *The Gondoliers*?"

"I have," said Wiggins. "It's a right lark. These two gondoliers become kings of, of —"

"Venice seems logical," I suggested.

"And they give all their mates high titles like toffs and that and make everyone a duke or whatever. Everyone's equal all over, like a republic."

"I believe that the gondoliers in the play aim to remodel their monarchy on Republican principles," Holmes said with a smile.

Sir Henry blanched. "The opera preaches Republicanism? I had no idea; I was not informed. This is a catastrophe (although the opera was Her Majesty's choice, of course). I must speak to Carte; perhaps we may substitute *The Mikado*."

He hurried off.

Servants bearing huge candelabra set them up on either side of the stage. I frowned and Archer stepped forward again. "Her Majesty don't like gas lights, Doctor, so we have candles and some electric."

"Ah, Mr Carte," said Holmes, looking over my shoulder. "I believe Sir Henry is looking for you. He has formed the opinion that your operetta preaches dangerously Republican sentiments to which the Queen should not be exposed."

I turned and found Mr Carte regarding me quizzically. "A harmless confection, Mr Holmes. *Pinafore* is a far more audacious lampoon."

I held up the handkerchief. "Mr Carte, I believe this may be yours. I found it, ah —"

Mr Carte took it and stared hard at Wiggins. "A wizened little fellow pickpocketed it at the station."

I bowed, and Mr Carte left us.

"Archer, can you get Wiggins here a footman's outfit?" asked Holmes.

"No, sir. All the Royal footmen are tall fellows. But I could suit him up as a page."

"Very well."

"We too must change into evening attire, Watson."

"The robbery is going down tonight," Holmes said as we made our way through a throng of busy servants and up to our room.

"Really? A jewellery shop, I expect. I am sorry that you will miss it, Holmes. Have you informed the police?"

"I have made certain arrangements. That is why Wiggins is here."

"Here?"

205

"Didn't I tell you? The thieves are after the Windsor Castle jewels, those of the Queen, the Empress and their ladies — with anything else of value naturally."

"The fiends!" I exclaimed. "They picked a perfect night for a robbery, Holmes, when the castle is all ahoo with the theatrical production."

"Perhaps, or perhaps not. In any case, it is our job to see that they do not get away with anything."

"We should have Sir Henry to lock the gates and double the guards."

Holmes gave me an odd look. "Why? We want them to get in, and we want them to get out. It is getting away that we must prevent."

We went downstairs at nine and stood at the back of the auditorium among the servants as the operetta began with a fine overture.

Archer sidled up to us at the end of the first act. "The Queen is enjoying the performance. She's tapping her feet and singing along."

"The Empress Frederick looks a trifle piqued," said Holmes. "She is quite bright — for a Hanover princess, I mean; she may have picked up on some of Mr Gilbert's digs at the monarchy."

Archer frowned and several of the servants within earshot began to stare at us and mumble.

Holmes nodded to me. "Come, let us see what news Wiggins has for us."

He led the way through the Castle grounds. "The private apartments will be the targets. The commander of the guards at the entrances has been briefed. You, Wiggins and I will watch the windows and walls. They cannot escape us, unless by balloon!"

An officer and a sergeant in blue uniforms stepped out of a dark corner and accosted us.

"Mr Holmes, sir?" He saluted. "I am Lieutenant Fraser, commanding the Guard."

"Good evening, Lieutenant," said Holmes. "Have you posted your men?"

"I have six men at the gate, under my corporal, sir. A fast carriage is at hand with another detachment. The station is closely watched by the Railway Police." He nodded to the sergeant.

"Two men in footmen's uniform went into the Private Apartments about an hour ago," said the sergeant. "The guards let them in as per your instructions, sir, and they will not interfere when they come out."

"Were they carrying anything?"

"Leather bags, sir."

Holmes nodded and turned as a page joined us. "Wiggins?"

"The Herr is in a closed carriage outside the gate, Mr Holmes. I sent Monty in, quiet like, to cut the traces. The Herr's not going nowhere in a hurry."

Holmes rubbed his hands together. "We must wait until Herr Ballater touches the bags. That is most important. With luck, the brothers will hand the bags to him through the carriage door, then one will climb up on the box as the other jumps inside. At that moment, we pounce."

He took a pair of handcuffs from the pocket of his frock coat. "I know it is ill luck to count your chickens, gentlemen, but I can conceive of no way in which Herr Ballater can avoid these. I shall present him to Inspector Lestrade with my early Easter good wishes."

He smiled at me. "Pistols?"

I handed Holmes a revolver. "The pin is down on an empty chamber." The Lieutenant checked his pistol, the sergeant his rifle and Wiggins slapped an evil looking leather cosh in his palm and grinned a devilish grin.

Holmes smiled at me. "Of course, I shall take no credit in the matter —"

I heard a crash of breaking glass and a shrill cry. I looked up at the Castle facade and saw shadows at a high window. There were more cries and screams as the shadows seemed to sway and dance.

"Come, Watson," said Holmes. He darted between the guards at the entrance to the Apartments and loped up a stone stairway to a wide corridor lined with tables of bric-a-brac and paintings. I started as I saw that several empty picture frames littered the carpet.

"This way," said Holmes, cocking his revolver. Lieutenant Fraser, Wiggins and I followed him to an open door. Holmes nodded to us, and stepped inside, gun raised.

"Hands up! Oh —"

I looked through the open door and saw that the room was a finely decorated bedroom. The wardrobe in one corner stood open, and drawers in a chest had been rifled. Two men in Windsor livery lay at the foot of the bed, and from leather bags beside them jewellery and rolled paintings spilled onto the rug.

A tall Indian in a gorgeous blue uniform and gold turban stood over the robbers holding a huge scimitar over one and with his foot on the neck of the other.

"Good evening," he said in a cultured tone. "I am the *Munshi*."

Holmes and I took sherry with Doctor Reid and Sir Henry Ponsonby in a reception room adjoining the Waterloo Chamber and watched as Mr Carte introduced the cast of *The Gondoliers* to the Queen. She looked radiantly happy, and, judging by Mr Carte's expression she had kind things to say about the performance. The *Munshi*, without his scimitar, stood beside and slightly behind her.

"His ship docked this evening," said Sir Henry in a wondering tone. "He took the train in all his finery carrying the sword that the Queen, against all protocol, allows him to wear. He was unaware of tonight's theatrical performance and he rushed straight to Her Majesty's apartments to make his number. He found our two Welsh brothers ransacking the rooms of the Ladies of the Household. He set to work with his weapon, and, as you saw, he triumphed."

"Are the erstwhile footmen dead?" asked Doctor Reid.

"Slightly mangled, bruised and very cowed," I said. "The *Munshi* looked as fierce as a Moghul prince in his turban and beard, and his scimitar is a fearsome instrument."

Sir Henry sighed. "The Queen is pleased. She requested that we form a committee to recommend suitable honours and promotions for her dear, brave *Munshi*."

Doctor Reid sniffed. "What the devil was the fellow thinking of, charging up to the Royal Apartments at nearly midnight with a scimitar? The Press will make hay if it gets out."

"I have telegraphed His Royal Highness, the Prince of Wales," said Sir Henry with a knowing look. "We will indeed have to form a committee, but our terms of reference might be altered slightly."

Doctor Reid put his fingers to his lips, and Sir Henry nodded and turned to Holmes.

"But what of the other matter, sir?"

"I think that will resolve itself," said Holmes, "but I intend to make assurance doubly sure." He bowed. "We will wish you gentlemen goodnight."

The following morning, a footman knocked at our door and a pair of maids laid basins on the wash stand and filled them with hot water. I was relieved to see that no writing appeared on the mirror.

"A carefully-planned crime," I said as I set to with my razor. "Thank goodness it was averted."

"I had the fellows in my grip," Holmes said with a sniff. "There was no need for the *Munshi's* gratuitously melodramatic intervention. We lost Herr Ballater. And as for planning, the robbers made a serious miscalculation: they made their attempt on an evening when everyone was enjoying a theatrical entertainment. They did not realise that, although Gilbert and Sullivan's works are not grand opera, one wears evening dress to attend and ladies wear their jewels. Their haul would have been higher if they had struck during the obligatory afternoon ride."

"I must say, Holmes, that I am coming around to your opinion about the Court. It does seem, *pace* Sir Henry and Doctor Reid, a rather dull and unmanly existence: all the dressing up and banal routine."

"There are ridiculous elements to most callings: the absurd uniforms of soldiers and lawyers, the abject deference that surrounds judges and monarchs, the rigid rules of dress adopted by the English gentleman (and of course by his valet). Pass the tooth powder."

Holmes winked at me in the mirror. "Do you wish to disestablish the monarchy, Doctor? Have Mr Gilbert and Sir Arthur made a Republican of you, my dear fellow? And in the Queen's castle — tut, tut?"

"Nonsense, Holmes. Equality is a noble, but quite impractical, aim, as Gilbert intimates:

To this conclusion you'll agree,
When every one is somebodee,

Then no one's anybody!

Ha! got you there, Holmes!"

He lathered his face. "Well, let us just be thankful that the French will never get their Republic settled and will continue to tear themselves apart every season or two; they are therefore less dangerous to the world."

"And the Americans?" I asked "Pass the towel, old man."

Holmes considered. "Tempered, and annealed perhaps by the fires of their great internal strife, yes, theirs is now a stable system, if corrupt. But, like all great peoples, like us, the Americans are romantics. They will soon imbue their president with the aura, if not the outward trappings, of monarchy."

"I do not feel excessively Romantic, Holmes."

Holmes gave me an arch look and I reddened.

"Medical men and consulting detectives have their feet firmly planted on the ground," said Holmes. He paused. "And yet, the doctor, detective, even the military man may dream of lasting fame: look at Nelson, of Immortal Memory, and our most famous soldier, General Gordon."

I nodded. "And what of Prince Albert and the ghillie?"

"As I said, with the *Munshi's* return, I believe the phenomenon would have faded away without any action on my part, but I slipped out very early this morning, let myself into the Prince Consort's room, wiped the mirror and wrote a new note with my finger in German: 'There will be no more messages: Mr Brown and I have been called to a higher plane,' signed HRH Prince Albert of Saxe-Coburg and Gotha and J Brown."

I grinned, "So, Holmes,

The Moving Finger writes; and, having writ,
Moves on."

211

"Well done, Watson! The *Rubáiyát of Omar Khayyám*, I applaud your scholarship."

"I found a copy of the poems in the bookshelf in the corridor."

Holmes pinned his cravat and checked his appearance in the bedroom mirror.

"I do not think we need to speculate on the author of the messages, but it was clear that she possessed her husband's key —"

"I say, Holmes," I admonished him.

He smiled. "Well, then."

I combed my moustache. "What a ridiculous charade, Holmes. The Prince's bedroom, I mean. The towels, and tooth powder."

"No, no, Watson. When I am gone, I shall expect you to do exactly the same with our rooms at 221B. I require that not a pipe, a slipper or a gasogene is to be moved. You may charge admission to those who wish to view the shrine. Shall we go down to breakfast?"

I chuckled to myself as I read the last line of my case notes on the Windsor affair, closed the book, sighed and reached for my cup of coffee. It was tepid. I stood to call for another pot, but instead I poured myself a glass of Madeira and sipped it, gazing out of my study window. The sleet of earlier in the morning had been replaced by driving rain. It was not a day for travel, and I had to abandon my plans for visiting my old friend.

I tried to picture Holmes, a stooped figure in the doorway of his Sussex cottage, smiling a welcome as I heaved myself out of the cab and hobbled up his garden path, but a stronger image overwhelmed me: Holmes in his frock coat and top hat in 1891, when the British Empire straddled the world, his head held high and eyes sparkling as he pitted his wits against the forces of evil that he had sworn to destroy. I sniffed and my eyes glistened with unmanly tears as I lifted my glass to Sherlock Holmes, consulting detective, the finest man I knew.

###

Also from Mike Hogan and MX Publishing

The Sherlock Holmes and Young Winston Trilogy

* The Deadwood Stage
* The Jubilee Plot
* The Giant Moles

A review of The Jubilee Plot by Davis Ruffle, author of the acclaimed Lyme Regis Trilogy and other Sherlock Holmes books.

'Holmes and Watson team up once more with the schoolboy, Winston Churchill in a dark tale of politics and political uprising and plotting. As with his previous outing, Mike Hogan's own plotting is second to none. The pace is leisurely at times and then grips hard when required. The book opens with a gorgeous scene between Holmes and Watson in which Watson is trying to do the 'household' accounts. He fails to bring home the importance of frugality to Holmes and that becomes a recurring theme of the tale. 'Take the underground', cries the good Doctor. The result: a cab! The dialogue in this opening scene displays the warmth of the characters to each other and Mr Hogan's unerring way with dialogue which is witty without ever being forced. This scene is closely followed by one involving Lord Salisbury which matches the opening scene in its splendid dialogue. The novel goes from strength to strength after that, plots and sub-plots fly by all deftly handled. Moriarty makes an entrance, still the Napoleon of crime that we know him to be, but with the saving grace of being an Englishman! This is the kind of pastiche that gives pastiches a good name. I am inclined to think it's the **one of the best pastiches of the last twenty years.**' [Mr Ruffle's emphasis]

Also from MX Publishing

Winners of the 2011 Howlett Literary Award (Sherlock Holmes book of the year) for 'The Norwood Author'

From the world's largest Sherlock Holmes publishers dozens of new novels from the top Holmes authors.
www.mxpublishing.com

 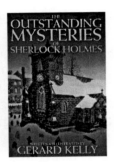

Including our bestselling short story collections 'Lost Stories of Sherlock Holmes' , 'The Outstanding Mysteries of Sherlock Holmes', 'Untold Adventures of Sherlock Holmes' (and the sequel 'Studies in Legacy) and 'Sherlock Holmes in Pursuit'.

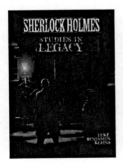 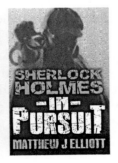

Also from MX Publishing

The Secret Journal of Dr Watson

www.mxpublishing.com

Also from MX Publishing

Two of the world's leading Holmes writers, Andriacco and McMullen come together for the first in a series of traditional Holmes mysteries – The Amateur Executioner.

www.mxpublishing.com

Also from MX Publishing

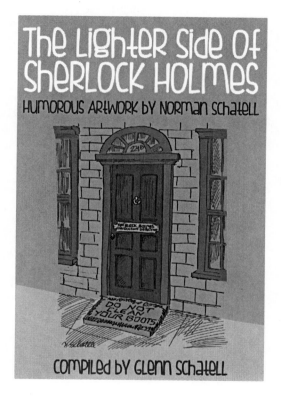

In paperback and hardback, 300 wonderful Holmes cartoons.

www.mxpublishing.com